TRIP WIRES

TRIP WIRES

SANDRA HUNTER

Stories

Leapfrog Press
Fredonia, New York

Published in 2018 in the United States by
Leapfrog Press LLC
PO Box 505
Fredonia, NY 14063
www.leapfrogpress.com

Printed in the United States of America

Distributed in the United States by
Consortium Book Sales and Distribution
St. Paul, Minnesota 55114
www.cbsd.com

First Edition

Library of Congress Cataloging-in-Publication Data

Names: Hunter, Sandra, author.
Title: Trip wires / Sandra Hunter.
Description: First edition. | Freedonia, NY : Leapfrog Press, 2018.
Identifiers: LCCN 2018010480 (print) | LCCN 2018013931 (ebook) | ISBN 9781935248989 (e-book) | ISBN 9781935248972 (paperback : alk. paper)
Classification: LCC PS3608.U594963 (ebook) | LCC PS3608.U594963 A6 2018 (print) | DDC 813/.6--dc23
LC record available at https://lccn.loc.gov/2018010480

Acknowledgements

"Against the Stranger," winner 2014 H.E. Francis Short Story Competition

"Brother's Keeper," *Mud Season Review*, 2015

"Modern Jazz Parade," winner Cobalt Fiction Prize, 2012

"Fifteen Minutes," *Permafrost* 2008

"Angel in Glasgow," *Nimrod International Journal*, 2013

"Radio Radio," winner, Arthur Edelstein Short Fiction Prize, 2011

"Borderland," *Gulf Stream*, 2006

"A Nigerian in Paris," *Reed Magazine*, 2012

"Where the Birds Are," *Red Wheelbarrow*, 2006

"Kitchen Nerves," *Raving Dove*, 2006

Deeply grateful to these glorious people:

Lisa Graziano, wonderful and supportive editor at Leapfrog Press.

Andrew Fairweather for the well-wrought interview, and for being a friend.

David Rocklin, Shilpa Argawal, Jean Hegland, Peg Alford Pursell, Cassidy McCants, and Jendi Reiter for rallying around in support.

My workshop family, Mary Sagala Marsh, Joelle Hannah, Nancy Pement, Crystal Salas, Julius Sokenu, and Christopher Learned who read a number of these stories in their first drafts and encouraged me to keep going.

My wild pink flock: Barbara Yoder, Barbara Rockman, Michelle Wing, Jayne Benjulian, Marcia Meier, Lisa Rizzo, Tania Pryputniewicz, Ruth Thompson.

Always and forever, my personal literary champion, Mark Sarvas.

And special "heart-deep" thanks to Andy and Aliya, who have to live with me.

Contents

Against the Stranger

*"Me against my brothers. My brothers and I against our
cousins. All of us against the stranger."*
(Saying attributed to the Pashtun)

6am

—You Pathan.

Heartstop and careful finger off the trigger. I didn't hear
him. What's wrong with me?

Skinny boy, yellow pants dragging in the dirt, head tilted
far back to stare down his nose.

It's one of those quiet deployments on the Afghanistan
border. We're on the outskirts of the outskirts. If we were
any further on the outskirts we'd be pants.

One of those bombed-out towns just like you see in movies, except this one has three-leg goats that hobble and chew
through the trash, and fat-tailed sheep with deep red furrows
ploughed through their fleeces. Some of the little kids say
nothing. Some of them shake. A lot of them shake. Their
hands, their heads. One kid's knee shakes like it's a small flag.

We patrol. Around the camp, around the village, around the
fields. You think it's completely quiet, everyone's inside, and
then kids appear out of holes in walls, from inside bombed

vehicles, from behind broken rocks, splintered trees. They watch us. We watch them.

We're here to be friendly to the natives. I give it a try.

—You speak English pretty good.

The boy waves a hand, like he's lord of the mud huts or something.

—You Pathan. Your eyes like mine, your cheek like mine, your nose like mine.

—I don't look like you.

—You Pathan. But you fight with Americans.

—We're not fighting.

The boy looks at me, the M4, walks away.

Where I came from: Chatsworth California. White rocks and cars hustling up and down Topanga Canyon. Chatsworth, the northernmost end of Topanga, where north runs out of road, becomes the rocky brown hills that spill back over into Stoney Point.

Hottest weather in the San Fernando Valley. Cool enough to have Stoney Point where the rock-climbing dudes hang out during the day, and the bottle-throwing teens hang out at night. Home of the Spanish land-pirates who booted the Native Americans out. Missionaries in 1769, Dad says. My dad, the history-and-just-about-everything-else buff. Mutters answers to questions on TV quiz shows while he's doing his advanced Sudoku. Speaks five languages, including Urdu and Arabic.

The kid's back.

—Come, Pathan, I show you.

Against the Stranger

He tugs at me and my M4, ignoring the body armor, the heavy boots. I could crush the small bones of his foot with one step. He pulls me towards the small grey flat-topped building, the *masjid*.

We used to go to the *masjid* on Tampa Avenue. I was seven and my job was to walk slowly with Dad's hand on my shoulder. We didn't go often because the hip surgery wasn't successful.

I stop. We've secured all the buildings, including this one.
—Imam says come. Put gun outside.
—Sorry, bro. No can do.
He throws his head back, doing his lordly pose.
—You afraid.
—Nope. It's just part of the uniform.

I'm a few feet away from the door. I check. Nothing moving.

The boy jerks on my belt and I can just see inside the *masjid*. He finally lets go and goes inside. Gun clutched to my chest. I can smell the cool interior, see the shapes of the people.

No one sees me. They all face the imam who sits on a small platform and begins to speak in Punjabi.

I am holding the prayers of my father.

A small boy runs to the front and clambers onto the platform. He folds himself into the imam's lap. The imam continues to speak quietly, settling the boy against him.

Early morning in Chatsworth. My father is kneeling on his prayer mat in the playroom at the back of the house. He chants, his hands at his ears. He bows. He straightens. Finally, he stands, his hands in prayer, his eyes closed, his voice murmuring. He opens his eyes and I can go to him.

He makes pancakes and flips them in the air. He makes one with a "T" for Tak. He makes one with a "D" for Dad. We eat them with lemon and sugar.

Next door, Mr. Windsor cranks up his Christian music. Dad tolerates the death and torture (*the emblem of suffering and shame*) but other songs make him mad: "I come to the garden alone . . . and he walks with me and he talks with me and he tells me I am his own."

—To sing about God in this way as though he is some . . . some . . . *boyfriend*.

Inside the *masjid* it is cool. *I come to the garden alone.*

The murmuring inside the *masjid* is faint.

The air is singing in my ears.

The sweat runs into my eyes.

One of my buddies finds me leaning against the wall.

—Fuck's goin' on? You dehydrated already? Dumb fuck.

He takes me back to camp and throws a bottle of water at me.

—Get your shit together, Tak. Lucky ol' Lefty didn't see you.

Lefty is our sergeant, with a habit of using his left knuckles to crack soldiers over the back of the head.

My buddies swear affectionately at me.

—Bastard standing there holding his—

Against the Stranger

—Fuckin' piss-tube.

—Lookin' for some action, eh Tak?

Dad says air conditioning is unnatural. Our house sweats in the summer. When I was little, he sat by my bed and fanned me with my mother's white silk scarf. It smelled like the sea.

We have a blue inflatable pool on the cracked back patio. We sit inside with our knees bent up. Dad says the Chatsworth heat is like the summers in Peshawar. The ice-cream-cart man who ding-ding-dings along Nordhoff is like the ice-cream seller in Peshawar. The women with the rugs slung over the wire fences along Topanga are like the women who spread their rugs out in one of the Peshawar markets. I learned to spell Peshawar before Chatsworth.

10am.

Back on patrol. This time I'm ready when I hear the faint rustling. I don't even look up.

—What are you doing?

Beat. A thud as the kid drops out of the tree.

—You not see me.

—Go home.

He lifts his chin towards the *masjid*.

—You carry dis gun but you not so tough.

He might be able to hide in trees, but the kid has no whispering skills.

—Go home.

—I myself can kill you. I have knife.

He pulls out a tiny broken blade.

—Have you heard of a quiet voice?

—*Dis* my quiet voice. Give me American candy.

—Ok. I'll get some.

He stands up straight,

—Hamasa.

Like there should be a round of applause.

—Tak.

I try a high-five but he misses my hand.

Dad wanted me to go to college. I was all for car mechanics. Good with my hands. But he wouldn't give it up. *All the men in our family have been to university.* So here I am. Books for blood, ha ha. Tour of Afghanistan, just across the border from Pakistan where I still have two ancient aunties and four cousins, all much older than me.

Sunday afternoons with the old school photo albums. Two faded women in saris and four untidy kids with mad hair and teeth-that-don't-quite-fit grins. *Even if you don't know them this is your family.* Dad gently turning the curled pages.

It's a tiny noise but I grab the kid and almost flatten him as we drop next to a jeep.

Cautious footsteps. It might only be the kid's father. How am I going to explain that I'm hiding behind a jeep with his son?

I check Hamasa. His eyes are huge. He puts both hands over his mouth.

I worm myself forward so I can see around the rear tire.

Shit. Lard-Ass, the unit incendiary device.

Against the Stranger

I have to ID Hamasa and me and hope he doesn't shoot on reflex.

Hamasa puts his mouth right up to my ear:

—We survivors. We stick together. Right?

—Shh. I'm gonna ID us so we don't get shot—

Hamasa jumps up,

—American! American!

I snatch at him. I'm yelling, *Don't shoot!*

Lard-Ass: from zero to 100mph,

—You fuckin' little shit.

I don't know if he means Hamasa or me.

—I walking, American. Dis *my* place.

—Get outta here!

Hamasa runs.

Lard-Ass strides over and grabs my collar like they do in the movies. I struggle to get free but he swings me about with one hand.

—Why didn't you ID? You a fuckin' pedo as well?

—He's a friend, not a sex buddy. You wouldn't know the difference.

Lard-Ass slams me to the ground. We're all trained to withstand pain. But this guy has to be 270. Almost twice my weight.

—Say again, bitch?

I'm coughing too hard to say anything. I turn onto my side and get up slowly.

He's got this crazy grin going on.

—Know what? You don't even look American.

He points a finger at me.

—Boom.

I look like my father. He says I have my mother's hands. I don't remember her hands. I was two, my father says.

She died of a gentle heart.

I don't know what Lard-Ass is talking about. I look like every other grunt out here. My buds call me dune coon. It's a joke. *You're our boy, Tak.* Yeah, I'm their boy.

Noon.

The quiet buzzes as I walk the fence.

A thin high sound. It's a bird's wail. It's a dying goat.

If you like-a den-a shoota poota rin-in it
Oh ho HO, ho ho HO ho. . .

Around a corner, squatting on a tree stump: Hamasa. Weird. He almost looks like one of the Pakistan cousins.

He waves.

—Tak! We survivors! Where is candy?

—*Jesus.* I'm working, buddy.

He nods.

—You no Christian.

—What?

He beams,

—Christian no say *Jesus.*

—Hamasa, your father will be worried—

He waves his hand,

—No fader. No mudder. Bomb kill. Two, five years. Many people die dis place.

The hawks hanging high above broken stones in Peshawar.

Against the Stranger

This is not my memory. It belongs to my father who saw the Indian planes, houses exploding like bad fireworks, people jig-sawed under the rubble.

This village has few houses intact. About the only building without damage is the *masjid*. These days, the bombs have moved on to other targets. And in other villages, other Hamasas are talking to other Taks about how their fathers died, how the restaurant exploded, and how they don't hear so good anymore.

Hamasa settles himself against a fence pole.
　—You don't have god? Everybody have god.
　—Not me.
Hamasa looks pitying. I want to smack him.
　—Den where you go when you die?
I shrug.
　—Nowhere.
Hamasa wriggles with laughter.
　—Den you die here and go nowhere. I go paradise. You stay in dirt!
Great prospect.
　—Listen, no one's dying and I gotta work.
He clicks his tongue.
　—You not work. You look birds.

He's right. I've been looking at the birds. Dad knows all the bird names. Crow, bluebird, hawk, and all those small brown ones. A robin made a nest outside our house, over the carriage lamp. All those little fuzzballs, poking their bald heads out. When the parent birds came to the nest, the babies sounded like tiny lasers. *Pew pew pew.*

—I'll give you candy this afternoon.
Hamasa beams.
—We survivors.
—Bye.
—You say.
—What? Oh, stick together.
He hops, pleased as if I've given him a gift.

2pm

We're patrolling the village. Life is one endless patrol. When I get back home I'll be patrolling our house, the street, the *masjid* on Tampa. When I go out on a Friday night, I'll be patrolling the bar.
—Tak. You come. I take you.
I'm getting used to him appearing suddenly.
—I'm not going to the *masjid*.
Hamasa flicks his hand in lordly dismissal.
We secure and re-secure these buildings, but you never assume anything. I'm scanning 360 as I follow him. We leave the main street, which is basically a wider dirt street than the narrow one we're on now. Maybe this isn't a good idea. I don't know this kid. Maybe I should go back.
—Come, Tak.
Checking: skyline, ground-line, any corner, any uneven shape in the road, by the road, a little back from the road. Any movement, any stillness. Every nerve is jumping and

Against the Stranger

I'm waiting for the electrical surge to go coursing through me any second now.

Hamasa stops, comes back. Tugs me towards a narrow alleyway, points to a small door.

—I can't go in there.

—Is okay, Tak.

—No.

Hamasa glares at me.

—Dis my *'ouse*.

Christ.

—Hamasa, man, I can't come inside your house. I'm not allowed. . . .

If his scowl could get any bigger. He throws his head back and I remember. He's the head of the family now.

—Listen. I'll just come to the door, okay? I can't come inside.

But the small door flies open and a tumble of short people rushes out.

Four of them. The smallest is a boy. The girls are 6, 7, 8 or something. They cluster around me grinning and shouting *'allo, owayoo*.

Hamasa hisses at them and they stand in a line. He commands,

—Name.

Dina, Asal, Maliha, The boy can't say his name and the girls tell me. Babur. He hangs back. One of the girls picks him up. She has a pink hairgrip. Babur has a pink hairgrip, too.

They want to touch my uniform, my helmet. I hold the M4 out of the way. They ignore Hamasa who is trying to order them back into a line.

I want to tell them that I have cousins who look like them. Used to. The picture Dad has is from when they looked like this, grubby t-shirts and torn shorts. Babur's nose is running. One of the girls wipes it on his t-shirt. They all talk at me like I can understand them.

They try to pull me inside, but Hamasa says something brief and sharp. They reluctantly let go.

—I tell dem you my friend, Tak.

—Hamasa. You're a lucky guy.

He pulls a face.

—Too much sister.

The girls sense his complaint and jeer at him.

—Tell them you're my best buddy.

I can see his chest puffing out. The girls laugh. One of them, maybe Dina, says something.

Hamasa clears his throat.

—Dey say you come eat for us here. Tomorrow.

I don't know how I'm going to do this but Hamasa looks so proud, so skinny.

—That'd be great.

—Okay. And you bring candy for dem.

4pm

Camp patrol.

Hamasa doesn't waste any time. Walks right up to the fence.

I grabbed a handful of candy after I made my 2pm report. I drop it into his cupped hands.

—Memenems, gom! Yes! I get many afghanis.

Against the Stranger

—You're selling it?
He looks scornfully at me.

My buddies laugh as Hamasa saunters off.
—They get candy from all of us, Tak.
—Sell it in the market.
—We're boosting the economy.
I grin and shrug like I know I'm a gullible idiot.
I wish I'd paid more attention when Dad was telling me about the cousins. I'll write him after night patrol and ask him for their names.

6pm.

Explosion.
Someone yells,
—Contact left!
We're running. We spread out and cover like we've been trained. We split into groups so we can circle around and cut them off. The enemy.
We're running along the village perimeter, trying to ID the enemy, trying to keep our heads down. We want to over-take them before they can do anything else.
Explosion. The grenade throws us like matchwood.
I scrape myself out of the thorn bushes. I can't see any of my guys.
Got to move. Got to get back to my guys. Get ready to run when I see this flash of yellow pants. *Fuck*. Hamasa.
You don't just stand up. You don't run out in the open. You don't yell.

—Hamasa!

I'm full tilt towards him when he turns and runs to me.

Explosion. The ground jumps up and we're pounded back against something that guts whatever breath I have left.

All I know, when I can move again, is that I've still got hold of Hamasa.

We're shoved up against some skinny-ass tree that doesn't give us any protection. There's a shallow ditch and I roll both of us into it. I try to shield him.

His breath is rapid. I can feel his heart-beat, hamster feet running the wheel.

I wanted a hamster but Dad said they died too quickly.

My breath comes but it's slow. Shock, I guess.

Dad says praying is what keeps him focused. He says prayer is his way of taking care of me. Says the craziest things.

When I write him I'll tell him about this dumb kid who doesn't know any better than to run around in the middle of a raid. I don't know if that's me or Hamasa.

Hamasa is staring at me. I lift my hand to touch his hair. It feels like he's dunked it in car oil.

—Wait—for the gunfire—to stop. We'll get—to camp.

My breath is weird.

He frowns,

—No guns, Tak. Dey stop now.

He can't hear the guns. Maybe he can't hear anything.

He looks down. I look down.

Blood pooling in his shirt, my shirt. All over us.

Breath.

Against the Stranger

—Hamasa. You're gonna—be ok.

He is shivering. He opens his hands. Torn afghanis and tootsie rolls.

If I could find where he's bleeding. You apply pressure to stop the bleeding. I know all about pressure. I aced the class.

He sings something. Why is he singing? I don't understand the words. I can hardly hear his voice. Maybe it's the gunfire.

He puts his arms around my neck.

—Tak. I care you. God love you.

—Buddy—gotta get you—out—

I can't remember where I'm supposed to take him. Out of here. Somewhere away from the guns. I can't hear the guns.

Dad would shake his head. Dad would make pancakes, one with a D and one with a T. T for Tariq.

Hamasa is crying. I can't hear him. I can't hear anything. He says something and I concentrate hard.

—We survivors, Tak.

—Stick together.

It's almost funny because with all the blood, we're pretty much stuck together now.

Brother's Keeper

He is walking. He is about to turn the corner.

She is at the window waiting since noon, since last year's announcement on the church noticeboard, last month's update, last week's email, waiting for her temporary Sudanese, temporarily in her living room, her kitchen, her guestroom, temporarily so grateful to her American family, American refuge from the dark nights of pangas and bullet mania and shouting, shoveled from plane to bus to this calm street where he will walk: tentative, neatly shorn head bowed, hardly daring to look at the numbers on doors, belongings in a cardboard case with only one clasp, limping from injuries, bandages beneath clothing, single photograph of family, bible with pressed flower from graveside.

Her window angled elegantly for viewing the street corner, her window well shaded but view unobscured.

It's overcast, just when Los Angeles should have looked welcoming to this new resident.

And is this him? But where is the pastor who is meant to accompany him, to make the introductions and—

This is the boy she was promised? But he is a man.

Smooth swinging chocolate lines, legs just ahead of that torso and those arms swinging, sinew to sinew.

White suit, white fedora tilted forward, blue shirt, blue and white tie. No one wears a tie. He is wearing a tie. Cuffs just ahead of the white jacket sleeves. Head up. Boldly looking at each house.

Tilts his head. She is there. He can feel her watching him from the house.

He is walking in thirty dollars. The hat, shirt and shoes are from the Goodwill bales delivered to the church. The suit and tie are from Van Nuys Suits You in the mini mall. He followed the sale sign to the one white suit behind a rack of brown suits. It is somehow too big in the shoulders. The two assistants let him have it for twenty-eight dollars (*You look like a movie star*) and threw in the tie for two dollars.

He looks carefully at the house. It is the right number.

What can he say to these Americans? What of his country can he explain so they can understand? How to divide the journey into language of *this, after, then?*

He sat in darkness waiting for light, and in light counting through the minutes until darkness. He faced blank tent canvas walls and longed for a few moments alone with a hand's width opening to the sky. He faced color, too much color, in the kind of geography he never wishes to see again, and longed for blank walls.

There is no *this* and *after* and *then*. It is all *now*. The rest stays hunkered, nailed shut in a blind-box.

He wants this American family to admire him. He knows

how they will look at him, this *refugee*.

The box cracks open.

His family is South Kordofan. They have lived in Laqa-wa for many generations, many families, many children. His father was a great man. His mother was. . . . His sister. His brother.

What would his mother, his father say to see him in such a suit? His mother's smile, his sister's big eyes, his brother's shout of laughter.

But, of course, they can say nothing: his parents are gone, his sister's eyes are closed and his brother is in the past.

Lock the box.

Does he look Sudanese enough? Perhaps they are expecting a dirty blanket and bare feet. He understands. He, too, was surprised when he first arrived in LA. Where were the ropes of chains and plate-sized medallions? Where were the gold teeth grills? Now he knows that those were YouTube stories.

The thick cover of grey-white clouds, curls and froths above him: anything is possible.

She steps back. Does he spy her at her lookout?

He *moves*. He could be dancing. He could be in a Chippendales line up. But he's here, at her door, inside her hallway. He's taking his white hat off and he's bowing to her, extending his hand. She looks at his long chocolate fingers. If she could, she would walk into that hand. She would snap off a chocolate finger and swallow it, feel it finger its way down her long throat.

Her breathing becomes separated: Howcan/hestandhere/

likethis?

—Welcome to Woodland Grange. I was expecting Pastor James. To make the introductions.

—He could not come. There is a new group. Some are injured. He sends his sorries.

—Well. That's alright. We'll manage. Good trip?

—Thank you, yes. It is very kind of you to let me stay, Madam Fields.

—No trouble. No trouble at all. It's no trouble. And how was your journey? Oh, I already asked. You must be tired. You must want to lie down. I mean would you like to see your room?

—That would be very kind. Thank you Madam Fields.

—Oh no. I'm not any kind of madam. You can call me Indira. It's a funny name.

—A very nice name.

—My mother liked exotic things. Follow me, Elijah. Can I call you Elijah? I feel like I know you already. I've read all about you in the conference letters.

He inclines his head. His head is the shape of an almond. She could take his head in her hands, press her palms against the cheeks. His cheekbones are sharp. Such beauty.

Elijah, the bold prophet.

—Elijah. It's from the Bible.

—Yes.

—Well, I'll show you your room.

She has to walk ahead of him. She would prefer to follow, would like to see him swing himself through her house. See him take up the space with his long chocolate limbs. See him paint the space in front of him, behind him, leave his wild streaks in the air.

—Here it is.

—How kind. It is a very nice room.

His soft smile comes from the wide black eyes and fades into his soft lips.

His eyes are hypnotic. That smile could dangle her off a cliff.

She says,

—Elijah?

—Yes, Indira?

Ind*eera*. He puts so much emphasis on the second syllable. Is that how they say it in the Sudan? He stands there with his soft fading smile.

There is a shuffling-giggling-shushing. The two children come in.

—Hello.

—Hello.

They speak almost together.

They stare.

She feels her mother-bright smile coming on,

—Kids, this is Elijah.

Smile fixed against her teeth,

—These are my girls, Blake and Edwina. Eddie.

Edwina, the smaller one, sucks the ear of a stuffed bear. Blake says,

—Elijah like in the Bible?

Elijah says,

—Yes. And no.

Blake frowns. She is 11, the age where imprecise answers are irritating.

Indira says,

—Well, girls, let's leave Elijah to unpack. Dinner is in half an hour. Is that okay?

—Yes. Thank you Indeera.

Edwina looks up at Elijah as she passes. Reaches out one fat finger to touch his hand.

He waits as she touches his skin.

The girls leave. Indira smiles,

—Your bathroom is just through there. You can shower, freshen up, or wash your face, unpack—uh, how old *are* you, exactly? Only the church said that. . . .

He is still staring at the bathroom door,

—Thank you, Indira.

He is used to recognizing the injured, the broken. The poor wear their wounds in the open. Those who can afford it use camouflage. Indira wears the flowing dress, the sensible ugly shoes, the makeup to cover the pale, brittle-looking skin. She has perfected her clean smile, her just-a-touch of condescension. But inside he can hear her need and pain rattling around and bruising her from the inside.

He can smile, too. His smooth skin. His clear eyes. His firm handshake.

And he sees that she recognizes him. She has smelled him out. She is the garbage picker, sifting over his body, picking out what she can keep, what she can discard.

There goes his white suit and fedora hat, his super-shined Goodwill shoes. And when he is finally naked in front of her, what will she want then?

She is the gate-keeper of his American life: his job interview, his driver's license application. For now, she must be kept firmly in the knowledge that she is saving him.

Has he ever had his own bathroom? She imagines him in there, leaning over the small sink, his dark swinging self, silent to the mirror. She sees the muscles in his arms flex as he leans over the small sink, his almond head tilting back.

He has thrown his hat on the bed. He has claimed the bed, the white hat sitting so jauntily on the pillow. Now he looks younger.

She backs away,

—See you in a while.

She walks to the kitchen and runs the water in the sink. The flowing loose water. Holds her hands under. Holds them down. Drowns her hands. *You will not.* Her hands dry themselves on the towel. But there are dried crumbs on the towel that scrape. She pushes the towel hard along her skin until it is reddened.

Her children come to the kitchen.

Blake,

—So *that's* Elijah?

—We're sharing our home. Isn't that nice? And we got him through the church, so.

Blake,

—I know all about that. He looks funny.

Eddie gurgles,

—Funny!

—He does *not* look funny. He is just a boy. An every day young man from Southern Sudan. And he's a refugee. How sad! He's had to leave his country.

Blake,

—W*hy* did he leave?

—We talked about this, remember? There's fighting and bad things going on. We're not the only people with a refugee. Aunt Madge and Cousin Poppy have one, too.

Blake,

—Is Southern Sudan a poor country? Is Elijah poor?

Despite the beatings he refused to carry a gun. They humiliated him in ways that crippled language. He carried their night soil. He cleaned their clothes like a woman. And they had other uses for him. At night they tethered him to a tree, like a goat.

But eventually, they looked the other way. At some point they assumed he was too scared, that he could only lie shaking under the small frayed blanket that didn't cover the back-bruising and rib-cuts and the dead meat that hung between his legs.

Praying that his brother was safe with uncle. Praying that his mother and father were watching over him. Praying for forgiveness for what they were forced to see.

And then there was a party after an important raid where they killed many. Everyone went to celebrate. And because he was too young, too afraid they forgot to tie him like a goat.

How much did it take to step away, waiting for the body blows to arrive? *What is this dish-cleaning boy trying to do?* What did it take to back away from the tents, not daring to look at the huts shaking with their shouts and laughter, to scrape and bleed across the barbed wire fencing?

Brother's Keeper

To run, and when it was finally safe, to walk and walk until his feet bled, and to continue walking.

Until he found another place, a city with cars and buildings and lights for crossing the road. And luck caught his hand: a family took him in.

He wanted to go back and look for his brother but they told him that the invaders were burning and destroying everything. *It is a miracle you got out alive.*

After some time, they brought news: the church would help them apply for asylum, and then they could fly away. Just like that.

Indira is irritated that he isn't as poor as she expected. She cancels the plans to visit all those lovely thrift stores on Melrose, the Macy's outlet.

Her bright mother laugh,

—He's not *poor*. Do you think he looks poor?

Eddie,

—Poor Elijah. He's missing his mommy.

Indira says,

—He's a young man. He doesn't miss his mother. He's going to make a good life for himself in America. This is a great place for him to start.

Blake,

—Does he leave black in the shower?

—That is *not* how I brought you up. We do *not* talk about people that way. You apologize this minute.

—Alright, I'm sorry.

Eddie sucks her teddy bear's ear,

—Sorry, Mommy.

—Oh darling, you didn't say anything. It was Blake.

—It's *always* me.

—Blake, you calm down. Let's talk this out.

—I don't want to talk *anything* out. I just want to *know*.

Children ask questions. Adults tell lies. He cannot hear what they're asking but their voices lilt upwards. Like his brother's used to. Did you bring me bananas? Is Ma coming home? Who are those men over there?

He picked up his brother and ran to the back of the house. Pushed him through the small window. *Run. Now.* His brother's astonished face.

—Go to Uncle Jospat. He will take care of you.

—But Elijah—

—Those men are coming here. They want to hurt us.

—Why?

—You must do as I say. Please.

—I want to stay with you, Elijah.

The front door being pummeled. Beaten. Broken.

—Run through the long grasses. They will not see you.

His brother's scared face.

Turned. Ran.

Elijah hears Blake's voice, louder. Defiant. Indira's voice hushing her. There's no point staying in the bedroom.

Elijah breathes in, pushes the kitchen door open,

—Hello.

Blake is silent. Eddie sucks her teddy bear's ear.

Brother's Keeper

Indira reaches for her good hostess voice,

—You didn't want to rest a little? I'm sorry. Dinner isn't ready—

—I will make dinner.

Indira's hostess laugh,

—Oh no. I can't possibly let you tire yourself—

—I am not tired. This thing I like to do.

He looks around the kitchen, her silver fridge, her silver toaster oven and microwave, her black countertops, black drawers, black cupboard doors, the black pots hanging from the rack above the silver stove.

His almond head turns back and forth.

How will he make dinner in this kitchen? Is he used to this kind of kitchen? Will he want a charcoal burner instead of a stove?

And what about the careful pasta salad she made, using okra instead of asparagus?

He turns to Blake,

—You can help me?

Blake steps forward like she's been chosen for the volleyball team.

Indira shakes her hair back, shakes off the idea of Elijah in the shower, his color dripping off him, melting him under the hot water, softening his bones.

She hates cooking but this is *her* kitchen,

—I'm sorry, this isn't—

—Please. Let me do this.

Blake,

—This is where the pans are, and the cooking spoons, and these are the knives. Be very careful with those.

—Blake, I don't think Elijah—

But Elijah has removed his jacket and draped it over a chair. He has rolled up his sleeves. The neat forearms and delicate looking wrists. His blue shirt moves in soft waves as he swings the long arms, those black eyes lowered to the gleaming knives, lifted to the pot rack where his long fingers grasp pots, one, two, three, each of them arriving with a soft clang on the range.

Blake moving purposefully now: opening the fridge, fetching sundried tomatoes, flour, potatoes, from the pantry. Blake pointing up to the colander. He hands it down so she can wash the vegetables in the sink.

Everything moving and swinging and flowing between Elijah's black hands and Blake's sun-tanned ones.

Eddie says,

—I want to do it, too.

Indira feels herself outnumbered, out-gunned. Out.

—Well, you kids enjoy yourselves.

She steps out of the kitchen, light tread, light hair bobbing behind her. Full of light and fear. Already too old.

A familiar feeling, a small shift: is this really her life? There must be some other home waiting for her. This house, these children: she must take care of them. No one else will and, left to themselves, they will only kill each other. This is her duty: to her country. Her country is motherhood. She must bear its flag.

The guilt floods down her cheeks, finger ends, elbows, backs of her knees.

How did all of this come into her head?

Brother's Keeper

Elijah unfurls. Movement puts the body back into the moment and the moment that is magnified when the body listens intently: the hairs just above the ears, the sense that the right eyebrow will twitch, the itch above the elbow.

The pots, the bowls, fly to him, the wooden spoons clatter. The kitchen sings its simple one-strand one-purpose song. And the children run to fetch and lift and stir. Elijah teaches them a song. They laugh. They steal shreds of cheese. He dots their noses with flour: an Instagram moment.

The dinner is good. Indira nods,
—So delicious. Is this one of your own recipes? Maybe from your mother?
Blake rolls her eyes,
—It's pot pie, Mom.
Eddie,
—*Pot* pie *pot* pie *pot* pie.
Elijah passes the green beans to Indira and serves mashed potatoes to Eddie.
Is he already so comfortable with her children, in her house? She puts down her fork,
—You know, I must, there are some things, email, I need to—this is just lovely Elijah, so wonderful of you to cook for all of us and on your first day, too.
Grates chair back, catches shoe on chair leg, clunks free and slams chair against table, laughing oh clumsy me oh clumsy me. It could be an aria.
Oh why did those words come? Pie like mother used to make in the old desert tent while we were running from the rebels. Now he hates her. Now he will never speak of his

terrible burning past so she can soothe him with her sweet support, read him cleansing passages from the Bible, sing old swinging-on-the-porch gospel songs together so he can hold her between his chocolate sinews.

A shocking image of his hard thighs and hips and his chest moving over her. How can she think that, he's just a young guy in a suit, just a young, how can she

Can she?

Elijah and Blake clearing the table. Eddie folds the napkins.

Blake,

—Don't worry about her. She gets this way sometimes. She has her medication and then she's fine.

Such grown up language.

Elijah,

—I'll do the dishes. You help your sister with the placemats.

Eddie folds the napkins.

Outside the window a black bird chases a bigger brown bird, snapping at the wings. The black bird swoops and flutters like an old oil rag.

Elijah, dish-washing, muscled, white t-shirt, dark jeans, small neat head bobbing to some internal reggae rap rock, same languid movement: behold I show you a mystery.

Indira at the door, unable to walk forward into her kitchen, the shape of the air shifting and flowing between the sink and Elijah.

Elijah's hands rinsing, stacking bowls, perching plates, jeans pressed up against the sink.

Brother's Keeper

What it must feel like to be pressed, to be held, hands lifting rinsing, perching her on the sink edge.

He turns,

—Indeera! There you are.

They you ah.

Who is she in *this* skin, that would go so well against *that* skin, would go so well against the side of him, so well against the back of him, so well against his white teeth against her, against her, his—

Elijah's teeth bared in the smile that points his cheekbones anywhere but at her cheekbones, lifted so-high cheekbones.

And the hot sauce dowsing her from up to down to up. Is she that obvious?

In the night, he hears her tap at his door. The door becomes a tent flap. Any minute now the intruder will come and take him. The tapping drips against the door, soft, insistent as though it doesn't want to be there at all. He holds his breath.

The girls knocks are much louder. Blake is one single *bam.* Eddie slaps the door with her hands *Elijah I want to come in.*

They sit on his bed and ask questions,

—Did you have your own camel?

—Do African people like Kanye West?

They tell him secrets,

—Blake hits a *lot* of boys.

—I can hit harder than most of the boys in my class.

—Mom hates Christmas. She says she's all alone now.

If it were possible, he would cast a spell on Blake and Eddie, turn them into something new and strong—like his mother, like his aunts who taught him respect and laughter and how to slaughter a goat humanely.

In Laqawa everyone would know about Blake and her fighting. It would be stopped.

Indira or her sisters need to do this job, but since he's been here not one of her relatives has come to visit. Where is the family?

Elijah is a rising bubble of joy as he clicks around Indira's laptop. There are pictures of South Kordofan. At the small table in his room, Eddie stands next to him as his fingers fly. He talks to her. The shapes of his land flow from him: how far you can see, how you can walk and walk. He misses the green smell of his land. He explains what it is like in the early morning when he stands on the verandah and looks over the dark wet earth. He describes the tang and crunch and cream of his mother's strange and beautiful French pastries.

He wears his white suit, walks into Sweet La-La Bakery on Melrose, tells them about working in a hotel in Kampala. (Uganda, Sudan, it is all the same.) They watch him make chocolate spice cupcakes; hire him as an assistant *patisserie* chef.

Indira backs away from the money he holds out.

He stuffs the grey-green money into envelopes that he cannot send. What address can he use: My uncle, my brother, South Kordofan.

He's been here two months. He has a job. He has money. How did he find his way, so quickly this young man? Is he going to move out?

Brother's Keeper

Indira knows she must leave him alone. In the long evenings she can hear them, Elijah, Eddie and Blake, talking, laughing. Children steal so much.

Rattling footfalls on the stairs and Blake comes into the kitchen,

—We're hungry.

The bright mother laugh,

—You can have some fruit.

—I want to make basbousa. Elijah says—

—Blake, it's time for your bath.

Blake's mouth chews itself.

He wakes to a sense of *weight*. Something is there. One of the girls must have come in. Perhaps Eddie has had a bad dream. Something touches his hair, his forehead. A breath: Indira. He tries to sit up, but she pushes against his shoulders,

—Hush. Hush now.

—Indeera, is something—

—You're sad, I know. Your family is passed on but now you are here. We are your family. We are here to help you.

—Indeera. It is late. The children—

—Oh the children. Must we talk about them? Let me make you comfortable. Now, Elijah. I want to tell you a story.

Her hand on his forehead. His hands gripping the cover. Her hand on his forehead. What is she doing? What will she do with the other hand?

—Once upon a time, there were two little boys.

She laughs,

—See? Not two little girls. Let's leave the girls out of it, shall we? And they loved each other very much. And one day they were playing and they walked into the woods. And then one of them saw a big, scary monster. So he screamed. Not the monster, the little boy. And then the other little boy said, hey you don't need to be scared. I'll kill him for you. So he did. Isn't that a great story? I made it up for you.

Her hand smoothes his forehead. Her fingers touch his hair, his scalp, drift down to his cheek.

Options:

1. Smack the hand away, push her off the bed, run out of the house.

2. Smack the hand away, push her off the bed, tie her up, run out of the house.

3. Smack the hand away, push her off the bed, tie her up, stab her in the ribs, hide her under the bed—

Smacks her hand away, sits up.

—I will tell *you* a story.

She stands,

—*Elijah*, there's no need to *hit* me. I'm here for you. I hope you're not shutting me out. That's what happens when you go through trauma. You shut people out.

He unclenches his fingers,

—Once upon a time there were two little boys. They were very happy. The whole family was very happy. And then one day the monster came to their house. You see? The monster doesn't come to you when you are in the woods. It comes to your *house*.

A sharp in-breath. She is scrabbling at him, kneeling next to the bed,

—I was only telling you a story. I was only comforting you because you're here and alone and I—

Brother's Keeper

His brother's big eyes his brother's small hands his brother dropping into the long grass running and running.

The truth comes rushing at him with a flaming axe: how can he be sure that his brother is safe with uncle?

—Elijah. Hush now. I'll stay with you while you sleep. Let me stay with you. Let me just—

He turns his back to her.

Her voice is different. Not sickly mother-sweet, not the welcoming hostess. It is bare, as though the wind has been hollowing her throat.

—You think I'm crazy, right? Crazy lady? I am *not*. And I didn't do anything. You can't prove I did anything.

She slams the door shut behind her.

In the dark, he goes to the table with the small drawer. Opens it. Pulls out the useless envelopes stuffed with money that he can't send.

He can stay and endure the woman's attentions. He can leave and be accused as ungrateful.

None of that is important anymore.

Driven downstairs after the night that has no corner to sleep in, downstairs to the sounds of the normal life that has no place for her, Indira comes into the kitchen while the girls are finishing breakfast.

Eddie swings her legs,

—I liked my poo smell. Did you have a nice poo smell?

Blake nods,

—That's because we had garlic chicken. I bet Elijah had a nice poo smell, too.

Bag packed: the money stuffed into his shoes, a pouch in his underwear.

Three loud knocks and Eddie comes in,

—What are you doing?

Children ask questions.

Indira calls from downstairs,

—Let's go! We're going to be late.

Eddie runs to him, tugs on his arm. This is the signal for him to swing her into the air.

—Elijah?

She looks up at him, her mouth ready to smile.

Indira calls,

—Eddie? Let's go. Right now, missy!

He knows Eddie is waiting for him to say the grown-up things: *Better go now. Your mom's calling you. See you later.* He reaches down and hugs her.

She stares up at him, eyes huge.

She doesn't turn at the door.

She clatters downstairs. The front door opens and shuts. The car starts up. They are gone.

He carefully folds the white suit and blue shirt and tie. They can be sold. He will remove himself from the room. He will remove his tread from the stairs. He will walk backwards out of the house.

He is a shape changer: watch him turn the stern grey-green men on the American dollars into Sudan's pounds with bright giraffes, elephants, zebras, oil derricks, pottery and drums. They will carry him over frontiers, barriers, through dust and thirst. And when they are gone he knows how to make do, to allow fatigue to overcome hunger, to wait, listen for his brother's voice.

There are more things to worry about than a sulky boy who won't come down and greet the family in the proper way, in the limber two steps at a time jumping three from the bottom way, in the way he floats around the newel post, his eyes half-closed, laughing into the morning. If he would just let her, if she could just reach. . . . There's no point thinking about it, the heat of him, the thick of his breathing, the pulsing almost in her hand.

Blake is whispering,

—It's okay. Don't cry, Eddie.

In the rearview mirror the girls are hugging. There's a smudge on the mirror. The smudge is a crow sitting on the mailbox. It bobs its head, opens its wings, cranks itself up into the air.

Modern Jazz Parade

If you will it, it is no dream—Theodore Herzl

In the dream Basem told himself: I am not dreaming. *Boom-lack boom-lack boom-lacka boom-lack.* This was the dancing in Noo-Allins, U.S.A. Dixie-music blaring over his shoulder, sousaphone scoring holes in the sacred air above them, people laughing, dancing on the sidewalk and showers of popcorn. Everyone waving and clapping. His ears glory-loud with trumpets and saxophones and clarinets, long, silver-throats tilted up to the sky, where Allah received their music as a blessing.

A strange noise curdled on, dragging at him, hauling him out of the US parade and into his bed: home, Hama, Syria. Phone. Stopped just as he grabbed it.

5:30am. Saturday. May 7th. Thirty-one days to the end of final exams. Forty-nine days to his eighteenth birthday when he could officially join up and march, side by side, with best friend, Ziad, in the glorious Syrian Army.

Two steps to the window. Checked between the sagging blinds. To the right, in about three hours, one neighbor would dodder out of her back door to pick tomatoes. On the left, the other neighbor would stand under her fig tree, pretending to look for fruit but nosing over the fence. Imagined for a moment he was aiming a sniper, picking them off at 50 yards. He flattened the blinds with one long palm. Listened. Mama wasn't up yet. His two sisters and Father would sleep until eight. Just a quick walk. Dressed, gently let himself out of the apartment. Ran downstairs and almost tripped over the small figure sitting on the last step near the door.

—What are you doing up, Antoine? Does Chef know you're here?

—*Ai*, Basem. No sleep anywhere. Chef is in the kitchen doing bread.

Head drooped against the stair railings.

Five years back, Chef Seroob found Antoine, Allah-knew-where, and brought the four-year-old back to the Hot 'n Tasty Restaurant. The left side of the boy's face drooped, two teeth missing on the upper left jaw, a squint in the left eye. The east-side Hama neighborhood sucked its narrow street, yellow-stone cheeks, probed its tongue along its rubbish tip alleyways, mumbled its cracked apartment building teeth. The fence-gazing widows, the rug-beating housewives, the chess-playing antiquities under the fig tree on the street corner. They found they agreed on something: the child had nerve damage, possibly trauma to the head.

Even if he'd wanted to Chef couldn't have answered any questions about Antoine. His only expression was the trademark *aaaaaoooo* that ranged in pitch and volume, standing in for everything. And Antoine, now nine, had nothing to say, either.

Basem fitted the MP3 ear buds into Antoine's ears. *American Idiot*. Antoine's face became empty, arms relaxed. He leaned against Basem's shoulder.

Modern Jazz Parade

Basem checked his phone. Nothing. Best friend Ziad: Dropped out of high school at 16, lied about his age, and enlisted. Sudden shock of short hair and a startled-looking stare. The Ziad who forgot his books, his lunch, his keys, was gone. In his place was a man in a uniform with many pockets: knife, cigarettes, phone, phone card, hand warmers, and what-all. And Ziad knew exactly to which pocket each item belonged. The Army had also taught him how to tie his boots. Ziad and his shoelaces: stuck in doors, caught in shop displays, jammed under someone's briefcase.

Basem and Ziad, scuffed-knees-scraped-elbows, fighting at the end of the street, racing across the back of someone's house to grab apricots from the tree, standing in front of the headmaster to receive six-of-the-best for banging their books on the desk in Science. Ziad's arm over Basem's shoulder, walking the evening streets, inhaling roast chicken and warm bread and *sfouf*, sweet almond cake.

Antoine held out one earbud and Basem took it. Metallica. *Where the Wild Things Are.*

Antoine sat up,

—Basem? How much does it cost to go to Istanbul?

Basem removed his earbud,

—A lot. Why?

—I'm going to live there.

Basem sighed,

—Insha'Allah.

Antoine yawned,

—But Allah doesn't pay the ticket to Istanbul. Come, Basem, I will tell your fortune. The neighbor-with-the-half-foot showed me. Wait here.

Antoine disappeared through the restaurant's side-door. Basem stood up and stretched, opened the front door to the building.

Morning light filtering through the lifting fog. *Rrrrup rr-rrrup,* metal shutters being rolled up, shop-owners calling greetings, shouting for coffee, small boys with small trays sliding past each other like eels. Ponderous procession of giant snails stopped, threw off their shells, and became kiosks for fried beans, green plums, corn on the cob. Two dueling cassette stalls on opposite sides of the street that sold virtually the same music. Each owner insisted that he, not that trickster over there, had the newest and best songs. *You're the one that I want, ooh, ooh, ooh, honey. . . .* Scooters zithering across the still-tepid traffic: father, mother, two kids and, tied on the back, grandmother holding a chicken.

Antoine returned and stood at Basem's elbow, looking up at the roof-top opposite for the kite so often birthed from between the drying sheets. *I wish I could fly that kite.*

They stepped back for the tall Senegalese pushing his grilled chestnut cart, and sat on the bottom step. Antoine handed him a small shaving mirror,

—Now, look into the mirror. You are going to marry Sabeen.

—What are you talking about? How do you know Sabeen?

—The one with the glasses. I've seen you look at her when she comes by with her mother and the three short sisters.

Grabbed at Antoine,

—How do you know who I'm looking at? And what are you doing spying on me?

Antoine jumped back,

—It's not my fault! Don't drop the mirror!

—It isn't your fault you're a spy?

—Eh. Basem. It's the way you look.

Antoine did his moony-eyed impression of Basem looking at Sabeen.

Basem swatted him on the shoulder,

—I don't look like that.

Antoine took the mirror and held it up,

—You are a big man, seventeen and all, but still you do this way when she comes.

Basem's face like his mother's: dark eyes, long thin nose, wide mouth.

Antoine said,

—Look at the nice eyebrows. Big and bushy. Girls like eyebrows like that. And teeth also are nice. Girls look for good teeth. But why pick one with glasses? This one can't see properly. How will she know she is with the right husband?

Basem jumped off the step and caught Antoine,

—You little—

—Alright, alright. She's going to marry you. She *will*. Ow, Basem. Let go.

Aaaoooo. Chef playing pan-lid cymbals.

Basem ruffled the short hair,

—See you later.

Sabeen, sitting behind the school on a low wall under the big tree. Black and white head-scarf. Black-rimmed glasses sliding down thin nose. Beneath the *burquah*, thick boots. Small, tough-looking hands. Didn't even look up as he passed. Who was she anyway? Their family owned a bakery.

Sighed. Time to go up these shaky stairs to the apartment

above the restaurant. The warm scent of baking bread. In the distance, the sepulchral moaning of the Noria dragging up water from the Orontes River.

Mama and the girls were in the kitchen. The living room door was open and Father beckoned him in,

—I have received a call from my old friend the Chancellor at Cairo University. I emailed your grades and last report. He agrees to waive a formal application. You'll report there for the summer term after your exams in May. That's all.

Applied without telling him? But he was going to join up in June. He and Ziad were going to travel the world. They said that foreign girls were shameless. He wanted to see that for himself. And how would Sabeen fall in love with him if she didn't see him in his uniform, didn't cry at the train station, and promise to marry him?

Sat at breakfast. Ate nothing. Mama looked at Father who asked for more *lebaneh*, grumbled: *These foolish demonstrations. Just lazy teenagers with nothing better to do.* Basem: unable to open his mouth, not even when his little sister announced she'd won a school knitting contest. As everyone except him congratulated her, she reached under the table-cloth and squeezed his hand. Felt his eyes grow hot. Grabbed her hand and squeezed back.

In his room, thought he'd be too angry to fall asleep but fell straight into the dream. Marching in the parade again, but the music was wrong. He didn't have the sousaphone. He couldn't walk in step with the others. He realized it wasn't Noo-Allins, it wasn't Dixie. People booed. He hated them all, screamed, *You're choking on a bad seed. . . .* Shook his head, long hair whipping, the crowds pressed against the

barrier, arms raised, faces snarling. Woke up. Heart banging.
Noon. *I must talk to Father.* Listened. From the kitchen, Father's voice sounding irritable.

Dialed Ziad: Ziad's voice,

—Hallo?

—You're there.

—*Eh, rohi,* I'm home. On *leave,* brother. A whole day—

—Meet me at Al-Hakkorah.

When Father went into his office, Basem slipped out. Just outside the building, he saw Antoine dragging the heavy trash can. Basem took the can and hauled it around to the back door.

—Eh, Basem. So strong and all. You should do like this when Sabeen comes past. Can we go on the roof to watch the kites?

—Can't today, Antoine. Tomorrow?

Lifted the small boy and twirled him around. Laughter. Basem waved.

The east-side: food-stall owners chatting with customers, café tables filling up with the lunch-time crowd, traffic wrangling for space on both sides of the road, two oranges caroming across the road from a tipped basket, three men crossing the road with a wardrobe, the door flapping open. Basem caught his swinging image in the oval mirror.

Al-Hakkorah, a hookah shop on the east-side of the Old City. You sat cross-legged on the blue and red cushions and sucked in the soothing combination of tobacco and mint or wild berries or citrus, the water bubbling gently in the glass vase.

Ziad was already waiting for him; jumped off the cushions and crushed him in a hug. Basem felt the muscle, the hard body.

Ziad held him at arm's length to examine him,

—I can't believe you knew I was on leave, you son of a donkey—

—I can't believe you picked up. Usually my calls go to voice-mail.

Basem looked at Ziad's uniform, tight across the shoulders, biceps outlined,

—You look so—big.

—That's what the army does, my boy. You, too. In six months you won't know yourself.

The waiter brought the hookah with two pipes.

Ziad picked up his pipe,

—This is special. Attar of Roses.

The dark perfume was overwhelming and for a moment Basem thought he was going to be sick. He was more cautious on his second try.

Ziad nodded,

—Good, yes? Strong.

Basem cleared his throat,

—You're on leave?

Ziad winked at Basem,

—One day. Got some fucking classified campaign tomorrow. We're probably all going to die.

—Aren't you scared?

Ziad put the pipe down,

—There's worse things than dying. Watching your buddy die. Surviving so you're left half a man and everyone pities you. Dying? Boom. All over.

Basem examined the pink and blue design on the pipe hose,

Modern Jazz Parade

—My father has arranged for me to go to Cairo University. Straight after exams in May.

Ziad stared at him,

—I thought you had to apply.

—He knows the Chancellor. Our family's been going there forever.

—So he greased someone's palm.

Basem sat forward,

—He just sent my grades and reports. They said I didn't need to apply.

Ziad shook his head,

—Is that so? Basem, You are such a child.

—My father doesn't bribe people.

Ziad put his hands up,

—Okay, okay. So, you're joining up?

—How *can* I?

—Once you've joined, no one, not even your father, can do anything. You're eighteen in, what, July?

—June 25th.

—So sign up after the exams in May. Get a fake birth certificate. No one's going to check. My father tried to report me as underage. Said I was no longer his son, and I don't know what. When he saw what the army did for me, he changed his tune. Now he can't stop bragging.

Basem looked down,

—All year I've been waiting for this. To do it legally. I wanted to do it right so he can't say I went behind his back. I never thought he'd apply to Cairo without telling me.

Ziad sat forward,

—I respect my father, too. But I also know that the army

is where I want to be. Basem, there's nothing like it. You're the best, the strongest, the fastest. And your army buddies take care of you. It's like a whole new family. Come on, brother, we made a pact, remember?

The prospect of having a new family was exciting and repugnant. What would Father and Mama say? But then, he would be with Ziad, his brother. He would be strong, somehow taller, like Ziad, carry a Kalishnakov, save his unit buddies. They would joke about danger and nothing could touch them.

Ziad settled back with the pipe,

—Listen, let's get some beer tonight. Get really blasted. So, tell me how everyone is.

Basem told him about the family, the neighbors, this argument, that marriage, this gossip, that feud. Petty, unimportant things. Ziad was doing real work. Ziad was doing army maneuvers, running with heavy objects and shooting targets. But soon he, too, would join up. And even if Father might be a bit disappointed at first, he'd understand in the end. Basem imagined Father's eyes shining with pride to see Basem marching in his unit.

Basem clapped him on the shoulder,

—Hey, asshole. Come on. I've only got one night. Let's go!

After an early dinner at Dream House (reliable for huge portions) they went to a few bars. Soon they were drinking and holding each other up because they were laughing so hard.

And then they were in a taxi, arriving at the apartment. Basem opened the taxi door and threw up in the gutter.

The driver watched,

Modern Jazz Parade

—I would have charged you extra if you'd done it in my cab.

Basem stood up and everything began to spin as Ziad helped him up the stairs.

—Can't go to bed. Gonna throw up.

Zaid found the keys in Basem's pocket,

—Shh. You're making too much noise. Let me open the door.

He got Basem inside,

—Good-bye for now, *rohi*. See you soon, okay?

Basem's heart blossomed with love for this, the friend of his childhood. Lifted both hands to bless Ziad, to speak of his undying friendship. And ran for the bathroom.

Consciousness came with sticky fingers plastering his eyes shut, poking about in his mouth with old porridge. Nausea rising. A slow progress to sitting, standing; slower progress to the bathroom. Rinsed out mouth. The urge to vomit passed. Stared at a face that looked completely untouched by the concrete blocks being thrown around inside his head. How could his eyes be clear, his skin look smooth? Surely something had run over him last night. Ziad.

Too painful to think. Back to bed, then. He opened the bathroom door. Father.

—Come into the living room.

Guts surging queasily, Basem followed and stood where he could lean against the wall. Maybe, the talk would be brief. He closed his eyes. A slap that rocked the head back, smacking against the wall. He fell to his hands and knees, shaking, the tears coming.

—Are you going to be sick, here on your mother's Anatolian kilim? Are you? You are no better than these dogs that eat their own vomit.

Basem retched. There was nothing left to come out.

—Do it. Do it and I will kill you with my own hands.

Basem breathed through his mouth. *Just get through this.*

—How dare you bring shame on my house? My family? The whole building knows about your disgusting behavior. I've already had Mrs. Doudan over, asking if my *dear son* is all right.

Silence.

—You have nothing to say? Drinking *beer*. With Ziad. And this is the fine army you want to join? Well, you can put that out of your head. You're going to Cairo, although you don't deserve it. I would throw you out if I didn't think it would encourage you in this nonsense. Your mother is hysterical with grief. Hysterical.

Basem lifted his head. Through the tears he watched Father walking up and down.

—Go to your room.

My mother. My sisters. Lay on the bed and cried until he had to turn the pillow over. Heard Father's voice followed by the clump and shiver of the front door.

The mattress dipped and a small weight arrived. His little sister stroked his hair,

—Basem? Did you drink beer?

Groan into the pillow.

Her small hand on his head,

—I love you, Basem. But you stink all over. You must wash.

The pressure on the mattress released. From further away,
—Mama's making lunch. You can sit next to me.

Sleep. Oh, to sleep. Pushed himself upright and went to
the bathroom. Someone (Mama?) had thoughtfully filled a
tub of hot water. He sat in the water and felt sorry for himself, and guilty for hurting Mama. The warm water felt good
and he soaped himself and washed his hair. Better. Yes, definitely better.

Dressed and went to the kitchen. Just Mama. She avoided
eye contact. He put his arms around her.

She started to cry,
—Basem, what is happening to you?
—Nothing, Mama. Ziad had a short leave. I wanted to
talk to him. We got carried away.

She put one hand against his cheek,
—Your father is so angry, Basem. Please. Go to Cairo.

She hugged him and turned to the stove to ladle a bowlful
of *makmoor*, the eggplant and tomatoes fragrant with garlic
and onion. Suddenly he was ravenous and sat at the table.

Mama sat down, too. Smoothed her palm over the red
Formica table top,
—You remember Amid? Yesterday he died.
—Amid? Who plays chess?

A small man in an old blue jacket and white pants that
pooled around his ankles. Juddered and poked his walk-
ing-stick way along Avicenna Street each evening to sit with
the other chess-playing antiquities; delighted in the frequent,
noisy-wheezy arguments over cheating.

—It was on Hafez Street, near the city square. Those foolish protestors were blocking the street, waving their signs.

The army came to send them away. But, oh, Basem, they used *real ammunition*.

—What? *Why?*

She shook her head,

—Amid was just coming out of the tailor's. Shot dead. Just like that.

She wiped her eyes with her apron.

—But it was an accident, Mama. A stray bullet.

—I don't know what is happening. We've been hearing how the army fired on civilians in Homs. Women, too. Not accidental, Basem. And I cannot watch my son being ordered to shoot his own people.

Basem stood up and tried to ignore the tears in her eyes,

—It's lies, these reports about the army firing on civilians. It's just foreigners spreading lies.

Pushed out of the kitchen before he began crying, too. Slammed the bedroom door. Texted Ziad. No reply. Amid was dead? Little Amid who always asked how he was doing at school, always asked after *that rascal Ziad.* Shot like a dog.

Tom Petty: . . . *under my feet bad grass is growing/It's time to move on/It's time to get going.* Ripped the headphones off and left the apartment. Antoine, on the doorstep, didn't look up. Considered stepping past him and then sat down.

—Eh Basem, in the army you can travel around the world. Will you travel around the world? Maybe to Istanbul?

Checked his phone again. Nothing,

—Alright, Antoine. *If* I join up and *if* I go to Istanbul, I will send for you."

—Hi five!

Modern Jazz Parade

Antoine craned his neck up, looking for the kite.
Basem threw an arm around his shoulders,
—We'll go up to the roof this evening. There are more kites.
The usual question,
—How big is the biggest one?
And answer,
—Bigger than you.
Antoine looked down at his skinny body; faded green shorts, Thriller t-shirt, brown sandals. Spread his arms,
—I'm a kite!
And then: the blasphemous shock. An army tank and two trucks creaking along, shaking the buildings and pluming up the white dust. The tank could barely squeeze itself through. People hanging out of the three-story apartment buildings, crowding out from the stores. Some child waved a flag. Some parent snatched it away. Basem stood in the doorway with Antoine, watched the tank grinding over old vegetables, old cardboard, an old street sign fallen, rusted, and now splintered. Chef pushed himself out for one look and *aaaooo'd* back into the kitchen.

Voices bouncing from window to pavement, from hookah parlor to mezze kiosk:
                    What are they doing here?
          I don't know. Ask them
                    Hey – what are you doing here? No one is protesting anything.
                    They don't say anything.
          Perhaps those uniforms make them deaf as well as stupid.

Ai, don't talk so loud. Those aren't toy guns.

What of Amid?

Yes, what of Amid?

Hush, don't make them angry.

We are angry, too.

Look at the mess this tank has made.

At least it didn't knock down any buildings.

I'd like to see them try to knock down my store.

You think you could stop them? An old fool like you?

Come here and watch this old fool show you what he thinks.

Now, now. None of that. There are children here.

Growling and shaking the street. Here they come. Here's the parade: one tank, two trucks with sand-colored uniforms and guns bulging out of the back.

Someone on a megaphone: *Everyone go inside. No one will be hurt.*

No one moved. A few spat.

—And what of Amid? Did you tell him he wasn't going to be hurt?

No one knew who started throwing the stones from alleyways. Kids, probably. None hit any of the vehicles. Someone threw a huge chunk of concrete. A warning shot came from the trucks. Women screamed and hustled kids inside. The men shouted, *Stop—don't shoot! There are women and children here!* More stones from the alleyways.

From the opposite roof-top, the kite carved a green and

orange arc, swooped down and landed in the dust. Antoine, mouth open, darted out to snatch it up. Held it triumphantly above his head and shouted for joy as the bullet kicked him between the shoulder-blades.

Silence.

Turn him over. He should not lie in the dust.

Behind, Chef Zeroob *aaaooooo aaaaoooo*. Hands like new bread lifting Antoine.

Starfish on orange and green kite, arms-and-legs spread too small; he flies now. Can he see the Sea of Marmara and the Blue Mosque reaching up minaret fingers?

Don't show his face. (Smiling over Istanbul. The blue cold sea).

Is that Ziad in the second truck, Kalishnakov across the chest?

Aaaooooo.

Tank and trucks grunting gravel.

Not Ziad, is it? Vehicles round the corner; gone.

Aaaaoooo. Chef rocking, arms like pillows. Antoine's body flowers over Chef's white apron. Chef covers himself in red flowers, deep centers. Antoine's flowers do not fade.

Basem picks up the ripped-bloody kite. *Aaaooooo! Aaaaoooo! Aaaoooo!* Chef swearing revenge. And the women with their hands over their mouths. And the men standing, arms stiff, hands clenched. Antoine, four feet three. Chef, mother-and-father, tears bleeding into the red apron and Antoine's red shirt as the ambulance arrives.

For five hours, people waited on the streets until Chef came back from the hospital. Ignored them all. Shuttered the restaurant.

Basem finally crept downstairs at three am. Chef heaped over the table, weeping into the wood, arms flung out. Basem went back upstairs and lay awake listening to the Noria's water wheels faintly improvising around Chef's mourning.

Dry eyes open to the gray morning. Whatever-time-it-was, Basem zombie-walked to the bathroom and washed careful-ly. Combed back the thick black hair *so like his mother's.* Avoided his eyes in the mirror. Shaved around the narrow chin. *Not square like Ziad's. A nice chin, Basem.* Gripped the edge of the sink as Antoine's face came back to him. *How big is the biggest kite?* If only he'd taken him up to the roof. . . .

Stepped out of the bathroom, slipped into loose pants and a clean, white t-shirt. Held out his hands and studied the backs and then the palms. Soft, unused hands Picked up a notebook and pencil.

Went downstairs to the kitchen. The scent of baking bread. Chef sitting upright with a mug of coffee. Basem tied on an apron. Pots and pans scoured and gleaming on the racks above the stove. Countertops shining. Next to the back door, the morning delivery: boxes of eggplants, tomatoes, onions, mushrooms, apricots, strawberries, and oranges.

Basem sat down opposite. Pushed the notebook and pen-cil across to Chef,

—Tell me what to do.

Chef stared at the notebook. Put out one large finger and touched the pencil. Looked at Basem. Slowly wrote,

Sais-tu parler français?

—Oui.

Moi, je n'ai jamais appris arabe. Peux-tu cuisine?

—I helped my mother cook dinner a few times.

Tu peux m'aider?

—Of course I'll help. If you write it down.

Chef, blinking away tears, took Basem's hand in both of his.

—Aaoo.

He wrote,

Mets les boîtes dans le frigo. Added, *S'il te plaît.*

Chef pointed at the three large fridges. One was for meat. The other two were for everything else, which is how they had been used. Oranges on top of lettuce, tomatoes squashed between loaves of bread, slabs of butter next to an open container of syrup, a stack of egg-boxes leaning over towards a huge jar of olives. Basem shifted the boxes of new produce next to the fridges and began. Into one fridge: moved the dairy products, hummus, delicate salad ingredients, juices. Into the second fridge: vegetables, fruits, jams, honey, and condiments. He checked for old or damaged food and brought it out to Chef who indicated what should be discarded or saved. He brought Chef over to the fridges to inspect them. Soft *aaoo.*

Next, Basem washed, cored, peeled and sliced the saved fruits. Brought out sugar and flour and butter that Chef whisked into pastry shells, baking 20 at a time in the two large ovens. This part took longer. Every few minutes, someone would rap on the back door to buy one of the loaves of bread now cooling on the giant wire racks. Basem looked over at Chef who was busy with the pies, and told the bread-buyers they'd have to give the exact money. Some did have the right money, some went home and came back, some cornered any passing small child, sending him around the corner, up the stairs, across the street for the right change. Many brought gifts: sesame cookies, pistachio sweets, a fruit cake, chocolate, baskets of flowers, vases of flowers, four flowers tied together with a dirty pink ribbon presented by two nervous small boys, friends of Antoine. From the roof-top apartment across the street, a huge blue and white kite. Basem accepted everything, thanking people, wiping his eyes on his sleeve. By the afternoon, the counter near the back door was piled high and completely unusable for kitchen purposes.

Chef cooked throughout, occasionally aaooo-ing and waving a note for Basem to read: fetch this, take that. Chef hadn't paused to look at anything, didn't glance up when the door opened, didn't appear to be listening to the gift-givers, the sniffing, the broken words of sorrow. When a group of sweaty teens, calling themselves Freedom for Hama, came to promise revenge, Chef turned his back and brought his cleaver down emphatically on a slab of beef. The teens left.

By the evening, the back-door visitors had thinned out. The last had been the chess-playing antiquities who stood quietly, held their caps in their hands, and gently patted Basem on the shoulder. They presented a chess-board with hand-carved pieces.

—You are a good boy, helping Chef.

—He will need help now.

They nodded sadly, smiled with watery eyes, and shuffled away.

At the end of the day Chef and Basem washed the utensils, wiped down the counters, swept and mopped the floor. Basem suddenly realized he hadn't eaten. Chef brought out a dish of cauliflower, tomatoes, raisins, and pine nuts. He filled two plates and set them on the table. They ate in silence for a while. Basem arched his aching back and felt a new admiration for his mother. The sadness came back. How was it possible that Antoine would no longer stand at the door, gazing up at the opposite roof-top?

My brother, my friend. These words meant something. You couldn't take them back. You couldn't build a maze around them, or bury them in the earth.

The side-door opened. The world breaking open in his little sister's face. She ran to him.

Basem scooped her up, feeling her small hiccupping breaths,

—He was going to bring me a kite.

Chef brought plates, spoons and one of the warm, apricot pies. Basem held a spoonful to her mouth. At first, she didn't respond. Then, the scent of the warm fruit and pastry must have reached her. She looked up at him,

—Stay here, Basem.

He couldn't even nod.

Fifteen Minutes

A freak summer thunderstorm brings a stirring to the dry, cement, river trough running through Los Angeles, brings the brown stench of rot, brings a grey sheen of sludge to the corpses of tires, car skeletons and, bent across a 1923 Eolan stove, the body of Omar Tariq.

The official from the coroner's office speaks to Mrs. Leela Tariq through a translator. They determine death by accident. Leela, who speaks perfect English, tells her cousin, Asal, that she doesn't trust the official in his sweating shirt and tight brown nylon pants.

Leela knows, Asal knows, that Omar jumped off the bridge into the dry, cement river trough; they also know why, but these are private, dangerous griefs, for the climate is sensitive to *these people,* who wear strange clothes—*hijab, burkah*—who do strange things—kneeling to pray on a mat.

Omar's death cannot be discussed with other trivia, like the Sunday papers filled with other momentary tragedies—who can no longer play golf, who lost the election, who died in countries chewed away by their bordering deserts. All of it will pass, all of it will continue. There will be small surges, a tide-pooling of anemone-like outrage that will die with the next incoming wave.

Farid is number three. The first was successful, they say. The second was brought down and brutally resuscitated. He must not think about the others. He must remain quiet and act when he is required to act. It is Sunday, no different from the other days, but he is proud that he can remember. On Sundays, he used to take his wife and son to the science museum, the concert in the park, the story time at Barnes and Noble.

His son. Nima. He feels his eyes prick. This is not the time to show emotion. But there is no other time but now. It is a blasphemy to parcel minutes out until they are gone. His small time will be over, but the rest of it will continue even after *this*. There is a despairing lurch to the stomach. Perhaps *this* won't do anything and it will all go on as before.

There is murmuring around him like a rumbling of agitated bees. But he is separate from them, corrugated iron roof above, wire netting to the sides, bare concrete below. Cell. An infinitesimal thing of no consequence until joined to others. But the others will not be joined to him when it is his turn.

So this is the meaning of time. He has counted two minutes and thirteen seconds of the fifteen minutes left. He stops counting. There must be other things to think about, more than this ten-one-hundred, eleven-one-hundred, twelve-one-hundred business. What are the other things?

Did Omar think like this? Did he curse himself, curse

the others, curse the enemy closing in so quickly that flight wasn't an option? If he hadn't jumped, would Omar have ended here, too, in a wire cell among wire cells? He shakes his head free of Omar who left a widow and three children to continue their lives, walking through their neighborhood before indifferent eyes. What are our children without their fathers?

What will happen to Nima? He has never questioned before. But he has never had to count fifteen minutes before. Is it not permitted to ask one question? Will he imperil his soul if he does?

Asal wears a long blue skirt and a cream blouse with bluebirds flying down the sleeves. It is her favorite blouse and it must be hand-washed in a delicate soap. If there is a stain, she must carefully rub it out with her fingers. A brush would ruin it. It must be rinsed once in milk, once in lukewarm water. It cannot be left to soak.

Nima, her four-year-old, circles her, pulling at the delicate bluebird sleeves. She smiles at him. She thinks, *No, please don't tear it.* But she is not thinking of the sleeve, or if she is then it is some other sleeve connected to some other shirt that threatens to unravel forever.

It is Sunday, nothing is planned and there is plenty of time for washing and mending delicate clothing if the need arises.

Nima runs around the house while Asal sits in the kitchen, then the living room; she stands in the doorway, waiting for the land line phone to jangle syllables into her. Her cell phone has stopped working so she cannot leave the house for fear of missing the phone call that may tell her Farid is well. There has been no such phone call, but she continues to wait since there is nothing else to do. Waiting, with its drawn out vowel, seems like an infinitely long word.

Finally, she picks up the cell phone and buckles Nima into his car seat. The people at the cell phone store must help her. Anything is better than being tethered to the house.

Five minutes. Farid is anxious until he remembers that it doesn't matter. He will hear the noise of the others creating a distraction. That will be his signal.

He can see some of the others. They don't look at him. The guards are busy, monitoring any eye contact, trying to gauge who, if any, will be next.

But he feels them: the one who limps since he was beaten; the child who, at sixteen, is so proud of the faint feathers of his beard, the one with a shriveled stomach, who should be at home, laughing with friends over a dinner of roast lamb and figs, the one who once whispered, *Inshallah, my friend*, whose black eyes are now milky and opaque from interrogations. All of them are praying for him, willing him strength and he cannot let them down.

Seven minutes. Long ago he relinquished the small corner of hope that he might see his family again. He has learned to keep these things inside where they are safe. Even when they question him, make derogatory comments about his wife and child, holding up the photograph just out of reach, he does not react, does not beg to hold the small colored square in which Nima laughs at something outside the frame and Asal's long hair, caught in the breeze, unfurls like a banner.

Fifteen Minutes

Nima will be five soon. They will have a party and the pink iced cake he so loves, even though his older boy cousins will tease him. Nima can already climb one of the orange trees in the back garden. He clenches a book between his teeth, struggles for handholds on the trunk, hauls himself up and sits on the lowest branch. He tells the story to the birds, breaking off occasionally to lift the book and show the pictures. For other boys his age, birds are target practice for sling shots.

Nima takes the same book, always, *The Runaway Bunny*. He can recognize some of the small words. *For you are my.* Farid's chest lifts, mouth open, to bring his heart under control.

Asal's soft skin. He once made a lotion of rose water.
This is for the body?
Just smell it, Asal. It is from roses.
I use this same rosewater in cooking.
It will make your skin even more beautiful.
What if I am allergic to roses?
Asal. Just keep quiet and let me put this here. And here.
He can almost remember how she filled his head with the smell of roses. He breathes in again.

Asal looks at the picture of Farid. He is so handsome, the curve of his smiling mouth makes her heart fill her throat.

She remembers the fortune teller in Teheran. *You will be a single mother.* The teller lifted one yellowed curved thumbnail and pointed it at the twelve-year-old girl. A curse. Asal would not tell her sister what the teller had said.

Four years later, she finally told her new husband. Farid,

a modern man tried to explain. *That's what our grandparents believed in. When you are sick, when you wish to invest money, when you wish to be married, when you don't wish to be married, go and see the teller. I can't see what the big deal is. You can gather the facts scientifically. This is what we must rely on. Science.*

He would know; he is a scientist. But that didn't help him when he was arrested and thrown into that place with the harsh name. She avoids the hard consonants, the bitter vowels. She can never visit him, never receive a letter from him or hear his voice on the phone. What does it mean that she has no words to explain to Nima? He still tells her that Da is in a meeting, Da is in the lab, Da is buying chocolate for them.

There was a time, she thinks. *I was a modern girl.* Now she is a married woman, with a child. And another one on the way. After her shower she stands in front of the mirror, looking for the four-month-old swelling. But the baby is still too small. *What is your name? Come, show yourself to me.* And, *Why must you come now?* And, much later, *He doesn't even know about you.*

Radio Shack's parking lot is being re-paved. They must park across the road outside See's Candies. She promises Nima chocolate later, and stands at the traffic signal waiting for the light change so that they can cross safely. She holds his hand, and he wriggles. She gives him a little shake,

—We must hold hands.

—But you are pressing too tight.

She relaxes her grip,

—I'm sorry.

Fifteen Minutes

He smiles up at her and her lungs balloon out with the joy of breathing. *Oh, let him always smile at me like this.*

The man outside Radio Shack rotates his arrow sign, flips it, jogs back and forward. He twirls and throws his sign into the air, catching it with one hand, one foot raised. There ought to be applause.

The man's movements are voluptuous. His arrow swims through the air, pointing up, then down.

The lights change and she walks, trying not to squeeze Nima's hand too hard. As they reach the other side the phone that doesn't work warbles a Bollywood ringtone. Asal stares at it.

Nima says,

—Mommy? Press the green button.

She does and lifts the phone to her ear.

A voice says,

—Mrs. Abaya?

—Who is this?

The voice is cut off.

Ten minutes.

Farid looks up. The heat radiates up from the floor, down from the ceiling.

He tries to think of a cold place. Iceland. He has never been to a cold country. He tries to picture the snow, the curving slopes of ice. He thinks of tinkling bells and black horses breathing clouds of ice-smoke. He thinks, *But none of that is true.* Iceland cannot be like that. Iceland must be a desert of ice where the wind blows as cold as the hot wind that blows endlessly here. But he cannot summon up this other real Iceland.

He repeats his prayers. He repeats his instructions. There is no difference between the two. Perhaps he should pray more. What if he mistakes the signal? There will be no mistaking the signal. He will have two minutes, maximum, to snare the noose, hoist his body up, and let himself drop. He gasps aloud and turns it into a cough in case anyone is listening.

And the voice of Asal comes. *Ah, Farid. You tell such stories.* Nima. Nima. Nima.

Nima stares at the man,

—Can I do it?

The man laughs and holds out the sign. Asal tries to pull her son away. She clutches the phone, as if to squeeze a reply out of it,

—Hallo? Hallo?

Nima releases her hand and runs to the man. He hands the sign to Nima who throws it in the air and catches it with both hands. He is delighted. The man laughs,

—That's it. You got it.

Thirteen minutes. *If there is one good thing I did in my life, it was to marry Asal.* She was too young; even at sixteen she behaved like a child. Most women that age had done their growing up. But Asal had mischief.

Her bare feet scuffed on the tile as she ran to hide from him. Quieting his own breath, he entered the room where he knew she'd hidden. By the side of the louvered closet, a pair of black shoes neatly placed together. He opened the closet door and received a hard, glittering shock of cold water.

Fifteen Minutes

She leaned back against the clothes, helpless with laughter, clutching the empty glass, as he dripped onto the new cream colored carpet.

He couldn't wait to get home from work. Sometimes she would spread a blanket, set plates of apples chunks, sliced nectarines, tomatoes, fresh basil, thick coins of Sopresso sausage, a basket of focaccia, and they would sit on the floor to eat and watch Charlie Chaplin movies. And afterwards, in a great wash of garlic and nectarines, they made love while she complained that they should have brushed their teeth first.

How much time is left? He must finish all the thoughts. He tries to concentrate, not on the memories of the past, but the ones he wishes for their future. Asal safely back in Teheran, among her family and his. Nima graduating from high school, from university. Nima with his own family. Asal with her grandchildren. It is like a comic book with bad sketches. Now this frame, now this, now this. All he wishes for is that they are safe and loved, as they once were with him. *I wish for you, for both of you, I wish with all my heart. . . .*

A shout, taken up, echoes back. Running feet. Rattling bars. *Goodbye. Forgive me.*

Nima tries to flip the sign again, but drops it. The man picks it up,

—Can't let the sign fall on the ground. Company policy.

He looks at the silent boy,

—You did good.

Nima turns away and walks next to his mother, who is still holding on to the phone. She is crying.

The Radio Shack sign man says,

—Is there a problem, ma'am?

—My phone. It's not working.

—It's okay. Maybe you didn't press something. These phones are tricky.

He takes it from her and punches the buttons.

She watches him, face running with tears that shine over-bright in the sun.

He says,

—Looks like the battery's dead. That's the problem.

She nods,

—Yes. Thank you.

—Now, don't you worry. You can just go right inside here and they'll replace it for you.

—Yes, thank you.

She holds Nima's hand, turns, and steps back into the on-coming traffic. Behind them, the man shouts.

The indignant blaring of a horn. She looks up to see a jeep filled with golden-haired teenagers. Words slur past, —*death wish*—

A long, green SUV slows down long enough for the wom-an driver to shout,

—You'll kill that child.

Suddenly aware, Asal hauls Nima to the traffic island. Her useless bluebird sleeves flutter against the hot thrust of traffic as it flashes past. Nima is holding her hand too tightly; she grips him back. A bus passes, a stinking animal of blasting exhaust. She covers her nose, unwinds her scarf and arranges it over Nima's face. He stares at her solemn-ly through the blue gauze. She looks across the road at the mocking red hand. Are they to die of exhaust poisoning before the light will change?

She turns and sees the Radio Shack man pressing the pedestrian button. He waves and shouts something. The traffic rushes his words away. He might as well be trying to yell through water.

She smiles uncertainly at him, turns back to face the bi-polar tide. The light will change soon and she and Nima can cross. The light will change soon.

Angel in Glasgow

An early lesson: the cold is a friend, stops the mind from reaching forward or back. Everything slows down into *now*. The cold is safe. Minoo lets go into not-feeling, stands outside Tesco's in the late grey afternoon. The air is fragile, comes curling in the mist along the narrow streets of Glasgow.

The Brechin Bar has evening warmth and anonymity, but it isn't open yet. She is trying to get the nerve up to go into Tesco where the automatic doors emit blasts of tepid air each time they roll apart.

There are electric lights everywhere. Wasteful light pouring like gold over the ice and the brown snow, running like jewels down sides of the tiled houses, the buildings, the bus stops.

A man gives her a couple of pound coins. Another man gets out of a car and also hands her a pound coin.

Things to know about men:

Men who give things will take things.

Sometimes men will kill you if they can't think of anything else to do.

Sometimes men will kill you if you say the wrong thing.

Her mother: *Not the children.*

The coins are heavy. They, too, catch the electric light. She can go into Tesco's and buy food. She stands, waiting for the next moment to somehow propel her into buying things, holding things in a plastic bag.

Here is a cold place with ice, many thousands of miles from *here* that used to be home. When she arrived, the church put her with a family: scared-looking old people, who offered her pale biscuits, honey and thick cream. She left after two days. She hid from the church pastor and his wife. She is ungrateful. She imagines them all saying it in their round thick accents. *Ungrateful gurrl.* She keeps to the corners, the edges where the snow melts into melting leaves, and the ice forms over, buries the tracks. She is only one of the many who were brought from Northern Sudan. She sees them, the pastor and his wife, walking with the young girls. Several of the young Sudanese girls are expecting babies and a number have become pregnant since they arrived. The pastor and his wife are always busy. They don't have time to look for the ones who slip away into Glasgow's narrow streets. But she can take care of herself.

New skills

Scavenging from the bus stop: A padded jacket with a

Angel in Glasgow

hood under a concrete bench. She picked it up, slipped herself into its arms and walked away.

Stealing from the greengrocer: Two apples and an orange. The smell stayed for three days.

A place to sleep: A shed with a caved-in roof at the back of the parking lot near the train station. Moved rotting coils of rope and a broken swivel chair aside, used a sleeping bag she found thrown over the parking lot fence. It didn't smell and there wasn't anything nasty inside. The joyful surprise of waking warm: *I have been asleep.*

Two girls, baggy jackets, torn leggings, denim skirts, platform shoes, clatter across the road. The girl with a face-chain that runs from nose to ear, flicks her cigarette butt into the gutter.

—Well, Tania's not *here,* is she?

The other girl has green-streaked hair and a stomach that sticks out from under her short red shirt,

—We're no doin' it without her.

Face-chain sees Minoo.

—Her. She'll do.

Fat Stomach,

—You speak English?

Face-chain,

—She's one of them Sooda-kneez. I seen 'em at the church. Rescued all these fuckin' Sooda-kneez, didn't they.

Fat Stomach eyes the girl,

—You speak Sooda-kneez, then?

Minoo,

—I speak English.

The girls go *ooooohhh* and laugh.

Face-chain,

—I thought youse wuz all took care of by the church, then.

—I don't believe in their church. I don't believe in their bible.

Fat Stomach,

—Yeh can no say things like that. Yeh'll be struck down. Jesus is watchin'. Me mam says.

Face-chain,

—So what's yer name? I'm Sheila and this is Kenzie.

Kenzie,

—Ah'm frae Glasgow. This old besom's from Liverpool. Loada shite.

—I'm Minoo.

Kenzie squints at her,

—Och, that's a daft name, then. Did yer mam no like yeh?

Sheila,

—It's no more stupid than Kenzie.

Turns back to Minoo.

—So you gonna rob the shop with us, then?

Minoo shakes her head.

—I have money to buy—

—Much yeh got?

Minoo opens her hand with the three pounds.

—Give us yeh money. I got an idea.

Minoo wants to close her hand around the coins. The coins mean crackers, maybe cheese. But Sheila takes the money.

—Stick with us, kid. We'll take care of yeh.

Minoo hesitates.

Angel in Glasgow

Kenzie,
—Ach, come on ye daft cow.

Minoo follows Sheila and Kenzie into the narrow shop, because they have her money, because there's nothing else to do, because there's a faint chance that Sheila will drop the coins. Kenzie moves to the back of the store where there are freezers of drinks. Sheila slowly walks between the shelves at the front of the shop. A metallic crash from the back.

Kenzie complaining,
—Whutja put them tins so close together for? I'm not payin' for anythin', mind.
Sheila waves a couple of packets of crisps.
—Can I get ma crisps then?
The skinny cash register boy rings her up and hands her the change.

Another crash.
Kenzie,
—Clumsy me. Wouldja look at that, then?
The boy runs to the back, red hands knuckling.
—Could you step out of the way, please?
—Step out of the way, is it?
As the boy kneels to pick up the tins, Kenzie straddles his back and rubs herself against him. He falls.
—Gerroff—
—Giddyap li'l pony—
—Kenzie, it's no funny—
—Och, Kenzie is it?

Sheila tenderly folds a bottle of brandy inside her shirt.

They walk to the front, Kenzie, strolls up from the back looking like she's ready to smash up the whole shop.

The boy is back at the register, flushed, avoiding eye contact.

—I'll call the manager, Kenzie. Think you can come in here and do what you like? You'll see what happens.

—Oh aye? Wu'll see, wull we?

Kenzie lifts her shirt a little.

—What d'*you* wanna see, Brad Pitt? Ma wee diddies?

Then drags her shirt up to show naked, fat breasts hanging over her stomach. The boy gapes, grabs the counter with both hands.

Minoo's hands are clenched.

Sheila and Kenzie hoot with laughter, swagger out. The boy swivels back to Minoo. She runs. The boy calls,

—Hey—you—the black girl—

Sheila and Kenzie running in their platform shoes. Minoo running in her flip-flops. At the far end of the street, they dodge down the side of a building. *Bank of Scotland*, faded black letters half-scraped off the old brick.

Sheila,

—Who's he callin' black? Fuckin' racist.

Kenzie,

—Well, she *is* black, then.

—She's not black. She's—come under the light, would yeh?

Minoo stands under an orange light hanging over the rubbish tip.

Angel in Glasgow

Kenzie,

—She looks fuckin' orange to me.

—Well, she's not *black*-black. More like me anty's new car. Lovely deep brown.

Sheila stares,

—Are them flip-flops? Kenzie, she's wearin' flip-flops.

Kenzie,

—Yeh feet must be freezin'. Yeh can no run in flip-flops.

Minoo,

—But you are running in these platform shoes.

Sheila,

—She's gorra point there, Kenz. Me feet are on fire. C'mon. Let's go round the back-a yours.

Kenzie's block of flats is a dark, fetid building with urine-washed stairs. Outside, someone is dragging an enormous bag of rubbish. It scrapes along the ground.

Minoo,

—It is only rubbish.

Kenzie turns around,

—Hawfwit. Whatdja think it was? Dead body?

You learn that the best way to drag a body is by the heels. You don't look back. You just pull until you reach the dropping place. Then you step aside and they kick the body in. And then you go back for the next one.

You don't look at anything past the ankles. You don't want to recognize the scars on the shins, the shape of the knees. You don't want to look further up and see the lacerated palms or the fingers curled up.

You do this in the morning when the bodies are still covered in dark, when it is cold enough that you don't smell them. Especially when they might be someone you know.

The grass at the back is a dry balding patch but it's clear enough to sit on. A couple of burnt-black bushes provide a little shelter. Minoo shivering. From inside her shirt, Sheila pulls out the brandy.

—Score! This'll warm us up.

They pass the bottle and toast each other.

—Winners, winners, win—ners!

Shouldn't they get inside somewhere? Are the police coming? They don't have guns but they have sticks. It doesn't take much to break bones.

It was a boy, a bored boy. And she made the mistake of smiling because he looked foolish with the gun that was too big for him. He looked like the boys at school in the class below hers. But a boy with a gun is different from a boy with a book. Enraged, he used the butt. She lifted her arm in time to protect her head. That was when she knew they were going to kill her, like they'd killed the other girls when they'd used them up. It had been hard to run with a broken arm. When she reached the Scottish mission she found she was one of hundreds camped around the small, whitewashed building.

But they set her arm and gave her the job of teaching songs to the kids for Sunday school. The pure pleasure, like being

Angel in Glasgow

shot through with silver: their out-of-tune voices, their habit of examining the ceiling while they were singing, how they tugged at their shorts or forgot the words. How they looked up at her and how she forgot what had been done to her. Until a man, some helper or teacher, came into the room and the kids went silent.

More than the brandy, Minoo wants the crisps. Can she just ask? Will she get her change from the three pounds? Minoo takes a mouthful. The liquid is harsh, but not as harsh as the beer that the soldiers forced them to make in the evenings, before they spread out the women—

Sheila and Kenzie drink quickly and pass her the bottle, but Minoo hands it back. *I drink very slowly.* It is necessary to reduce the heart-beat. It is necessary to breathe the heart back to normal.

Kenzie nods, swallows.

—Yer first time robbin'? I was skerrit ma firs' time.

Then brays.

—I wasnae! No one fucks wi' me.

—Shurrup, Kenzie. She's not used to it.

Kenzie hangs over Minoo. Minoo counts: One-one-hundred, two-one-hundred, three-one-hundred.

—You should do somethin' about yersel'. Hey—

Kenzie turns to Sheila.

—Less give 'er a do!

Sheila puts an arm out.

—Yer bevvied.

—Am no.

Sandra Hunter

Kenzie roots in her bag and pulls out a small pair of scissors,
—Come on, Soo-dan. Ah-ll mek yeh look gor-gee-uss.
She snaps the scissors in the air.

Minoo breathes. Fifteen-one-hundred. Sixteen-one-hundred.
It's never an attack until—
Sheila tries to wrench the scissors away but Kenzie shoves
and Sheila falls backwards. Kenzie with the scissors jawing
open and shut. Laughing.
Minoo counts. Twenty-two-one-hundred. Twenty-three-
one-hundred.

Sheila tries to grab at Kenzie's legs, but Kenzie swoops forward, the scissors rasping. Kneels in front of Minoo. Snips a
chunk of hair. Stares. Laughs, looks over her shoulder.
—She let me do it! Wouldja believe it?

There is no time to decide whether to move or not to move.
Minoo stabs rigid fingers into the solar plexus. Kenzie
buckles, gurgling, heaving on the bald earth.
No time to decide.
Minoo snatches the scissors, closes the blades and aims
straight for the neck.
Sheila's platform shoe connects with Minoo's hand and
the scissors drop, hitting Kenzie on the temple.

Kenzie gasping,
—Bitch! I'll fuckin' kill yeh!
Sheila looks at Minoo.

Angel in Glasgow

—*Go.*

Minoo, on her feet, backs away, wants to run but can't.

Kenzie staggers upright. Aims a punch at Sheila and misses.

—Kenzie!

A new voice. Male. The black hooded outline approaches. Hands stuffed in his hoodie pouch pocket.

There is no decision to move. Instantly, the scissors are in Minoo's hand, blades forward. He won't be able to get anywhere near. If she just runs now. If she just runs. The feet don't move. Scissors pointing out.

Kenzie coughs.

—Fuck're *yü* doin' here?

—Just got off. Y'know.

It is the boy from Tesco's. He stands there, the hands fumbling in his pockets like they're trying to escape.

—Thought you'd come down here for a quick one, didja?

—Kenzie, it's not like that.

The boy moves closer. Kenzie's face has changed. Softer. She smiles a little. Looks at the boy from the wild scourings of eyeliner.

—Och, c'mon then.

He helps Kenzie to her feet. Picks up her bag. They walk off together. She doesn't look around or say goodbye.

Sheila sighs, picks up the half-full bottle of brandy.

Minoo,

—This is her boyfriend?

—She goes with him sometimes.

91

Beat.

—I want my change.

—Wha'?

—My change. You took my three pounds.

Sheila rummages in her pocket and hands over coins.

—C'mon. Let's go the pub.

I want the crisps.

The alcohol is thrumming in her chest, her stomach. Heart banging from the attack that wasn't an attack. The rules are different here.

Sheila,

—Look at the state of them feet.

Minoo looks down at the pale green flip flops against the dark skin, black toe-nails.

—Yes.

—Yeh gorra get some shoes.

They head back along Govan Road and push into the Brechin Bar. Old men at the bar, pool table busy, young guys standing in shouldered-off groups, groups of girls sitting around small tables. Bartender swinging glasses down from the rack above, calling an order over his shoulder. *What's yours?* The tall dark beer glasses, short pale glasses of gold gleaming on the dark wood.

Sheila digs in her pockets and pulls out coins.

—Giss the money. C'mon. It's for the drinks.

Minoo hands back her change.

—We got enough for a couple of 'alves. Wait 'ere.

Angel in Glasgow

Minoo stands near the door, back against the wall. The police won't come now. But even so, her heart is juddering, beating its own time in a way she remembers. *Out, get out, out, get out.*

Sheila comes back with half-pints of a pale liquid and they head to the small room at the back where the noise falls away.

Back against the wall, facing the doorway, Minoo holds the cold glass in cold hands, stares into the condensation. Trickles clear small, winding paths. That one is hers. The one that stops suddenly is her mother's. Her brothers, her father, the baby.

Sheila swallows a mouthful.

—I suppose it's none of me business, but what really happened over there? How come yez all had to leave? They all murderin' yez, like?

Minoo releases the glass.

—I'm from Kosti. It is a big town in North Sudan. It is below Khartoum. Do you know Khartoum?

—I saw that Sudan on the telly. Africa, righ'? I love them beads you lot put in yer hair, yeh?

Minoo was once one of those girls on the telly. She and her mother fetched firewood and balanced 15-gallon jerry cans of water on their heads. Each night her mother braided her hair. That was before the soldiers came.

—So did them church lot come and save yez?

The glass of beer: pale gold running with tears.

—Those church people tell lies. They tell lies to us in our country and they tell lies to us in this country. And then the girls are pregnant.

—Yeh. It's always the fuckin' men.

Sheila tips the beer back. As she swallows, Minoo sees a thin, pale line across the left side of the throat.

—Someone cut you?

She gestures to Sheila's throat.

—Yeh. Me dad. Got pregnant off his best friend, didn't I?

—But—his friend—

—Don't remember nottin'. Drunk, wasn't I? Me dad went mad. Lucky me mam stopped him.

Minoo is silent. Everything tumbles like a bad movie. Purple-white lights in Tesco's, scissors, brandy, cold blank sky, a man cutting his daughter's throat.

Screech and bellow as something is murdered in the bar. Sheila's eyebrows hitch, one pierced with a silver stud.

—That'll be the karaoke. You ever done the karaoke? C'mon. It'll be a great cultural experience.

She was looking at me, yeh, me, and I could tell it wouldn't be long. . . .

In the bar people shout above the music. Girls draped around each other, *me, yeh, me.* Explosions of laughter. Cheering. The men are shouting almost louder than the small, middle-aged man with a microphone right up to his yellow teeth.

Ah love rocknroll put another dam in the jukebox baby

Angel in Glasgow

—Let's us have a go, eh? You an' me could sing something, yeh?

Sheila pushes to the front and says something to a bearded man with a clipboard. He nods. Sheila comes back.

—We're on next. You ready?

Minoo looks around for the door.

—I don't know these songs—

—It doesn't matter. Just follow along.

—But I—

—You can sing, righ'? Everyone can sing.

—What?

The music is terrible, painful, blistering. The song ends and cheers overtake any remaining conversation. Laughter.

Her mother and father, her three brothers, sitting on stools, everyone laughing because they have eaten. Her brother has washed the utensils. Mother said, *He will make a fine husband.* And they all laughed. And her stomach was warm.

A girl in a short skirt sings, loud, earnest, flat. And then Sheila is tugging on her arm.

—It's us.

Ooze.

The grinning faces gel, congeal, melt, pull apart. She can't tell if they're friendly or not. Sheila holds on to her sleeve as someone slurs,

—*Whurr dya find thus one?*

Sheila shouts over the music,

—Ignore them. Ignorant load of shite. There's the screen. Just sing along.

The blue screen begins to scroll words. Minoo looks at Sheila who starts to sing over a chirpy steel guitar.

—*Ah trad so hard my dear to show that yer mah every dream, yet yer afraid each thing ah do is just some evil scheme. . . .*

Sheila nods at her. Minoo looks back at the screen. Her tongue is frozen. Someone shouts,

—C'mon, hen. Sing!

Minoo opens her mouth and whispers,

—*keep us so far apart—*

And is saved by the roar of the crowd,

Why can't I free yer doubtful mahnd and melt yer cold cold heart.

She stares hard at the blue screen, mic in a death grip. When will it end? They get to the *cold cold heart* line again and a big man with a thick, red beard, bellows along, a few words behind. This echoing effect makes the song even longer than it is. Minoo watches the man sing, his head up, eyes squeezed shut, and his pint of beer clutched to his belly.

As she finishes the song, she is weeping. The man opens his eyes. His face and neck are running with sweat. Even his pale-gold eyebrows are damp. He stares at her, through the cheering, the clapping, the whistles.

The memory of smell:

Her mother: wood smoke, a sweet smell, body lotion.

Her father: oil, cigarette smoke, the cold of being outdoors.

Her brothers: dirt, trees, small-boy sweat.

Her sister: baby hair.

Angel in Glasgow

When the memory of smell goes that's when the person begins to fade.

In the dream, she tells herself to stay awake to remember. As she breathes, their voices come back, their bodies flicker in the firelight, they move the air around them and she can feel how they *are. We are well. You will not leave us. We don't think you can forget us.*

Someone says,

—Even the wee black one's cryin'. God love 'er.

The red bearded man strides across to the stage and holds out his hand. Minoo takes it, steps down, and he leads her to a corner of the bar.

He orders two whiskeys and places one in front of her.

Nods his head. They clink glasses. He leans forward.

—Yeh sing like 'n angel.

—Thank you. I saw you singing, too.

—Ma wife. She took the young 'uns aff tae Manchester. Might as well be Africa—no offense. Eight years ago. She can rot in hail, the auld besom. It's the kids. I miss ma kids.

He knocks the whiskey back.

—Ye got family?

—Dead.

She surprises herself with the Scots accent: *deid.*

He nods.

—Bastards. In the war were ye? Hurd about tha'.

—Aye.

The Scots word comes suddenly, easily. Her mouth can do new things. She can sing. She can speak the Scottish language.

He nods again.

—Aye. Them as done the war, they got it comin', angel. Don't you worry. They got it comin' bug time.

He tilts his head,

—Angel. Guid name for ye.

Points at her hair.

—Y'even got a wee halo.

She lifts a hand to touch her hair. Halo.

—Ma name's Preston Robert, but everyone calls me Pirate. It's tha beard.

—It's a good name. Pirate.

—Naice the way ye say it. Pi-rate.

Sheila arrives.

—Y'alright, hen?

—This is Pirate.

—A pirate are yeh? And what're youse sayin' to me mate?

—I was complimentin' yer friend on her sung'n'. Ye're nae bad yersel'.

Sheila grins,

—Well, thanks, then.

He raises his glass to Minoo,

—Ah hope ta see ye once again, Miss Minoo.

He shuffles away.

Sheila rolls her eyes at Minoo.

—The state of 'im. C'mon. Less geroff home.

They leave the broken karaoke hearts behind and walk out into Glasgow's narrow streets. Sheila talks about some shoes she can give Minoo. Pink trainers.

Angel in Glasgow

—They're not new, but they'll keep yer feet warm.

The mist has come swirling back. Sheila turns off onto another street before Dalreoch Station.

—Well, this is me, then. Yeh gonna be alrigh'? Gorra place to stay, like?

—Yes, thank you. My place is not far.

Minoo hesitates,

—I had a good time. You are a nice gurrl, Sheila.

Sheila laughs,

—I see yer pickin' up the accent. Very nice. Come round the pub t'morrer nigh'. I'll bring them shoes.

Minoo walks through the curling Glasgow mist to Dalreoch Station. Beneath her hiding place, a loose pile of chipped bricks and wooden palings, she finds her sleeping bag and the Seventeen magazine she lifted from Tesco's a week ago. She slips between the splintered walls of the broken shed. There's a faint glow from an orange light in the parking lot. She opens her magazine and finds the fashion advice. *It's time to put away those summer shoes. Make sure you store them properly.*

What would it be like to be so rich that you could have shoes for each season of the year?

A scuffling and sliding close by. A tin can, goes bouncing across the parking lot. She shoves the magazines and sleeping bag beneath a loose plank. She wedges herself behind a broken piece of hardboard.

It might be the Scavenger Man, the one who collects empty

bottles. She has watched him pick patiently through torn pieces of paper, searching for a number, a sequence of letters that make sense. It might be bored boys looking for a distraction. It might be someone with too much time and not enough sleep.

The orange parking lot light is too faint to reflect the sweet-bright shine of the scissors in her hand, blades forward.

Radio Radio

And here's Adriana singing just for you.

But this is not the famous *Voces del Secuestro* radio station, and this isn't Colombia. And I am not sitting on some scrap of canvas or drinking coffee or wondering when I'll get a chance to shave. I am not expecting to grab my cloth bag with the notebook and pen, the dry highlighter, the small tin that used to hold mints. I am not walking through long wet grass that whips my face. I am not stumbling across the ankle-bending rocks in a dry river bed. Muffled words are not shouted from behind a green scarf, and I am not clubbed to the ground because I didn't know I was being told to lie down. I am not being slapped across the face because I looked up at the wrong moment. I am not thinking, *This is not me in this body in this place forced to walk and squat, to be pushed around with the muzzle of a gun.*

One of the youngest Green Masks, a kid with pants rolled up around the ankles, was pushing Elsa around with the gun and it went off. His face came undone. *It was a mistake.* We all watched as she fell, just dropped out of the living moment, and her shirt grew red hibiscus flowers. And then she twisted onto her side, slipped out of her open eyes. The other Green Masks shouted. One of them hit the kid. Some of us were crying because we were all we had left and now we were fewer. But none of us went to Elsa, whose red shirt made the wet grass blacker than her hair.

I am not dead.

I am.

I am someone who listens to the radio.

We left Elsa in the wet grass and no one looked back. Some of the green masks stayed behind. Maybe they buried her. We went on walking. I thought they were leading us in a circle back to the place we'd just been. But when we got there it was different even though there were the same bushes and trees. The hut for the outside toilet had no door.

Lobo was dead for a day before the Green Masks noticed. We didn't say anything. We were all we had left. We were angry with Lobo, but sad because he had diabetes and no medication. Well. He warned them. I took his glasses case. Lobo was a scientist. His voice played low notes and his pale eyes blinked through the wire-rimmed glasses. He talked about soil nutrients in the late evenings when I longed to see the sky. I didn't mean to steal from him. I just wanted to keep him with me. But the others stopped talking to me after that. They turned their backs. Sometimes I'd stand near the window to watch the Green Masks sitting or lazily wrestling or cleaning their guns. I prayed a lot. Dear God, let the others talk to me again. Let them forgive me as I have forgiven the Green Masks.

When I raise my glass I salute those people, the ones who are still there.

Radio Radio

That part wasn't true. I didn't forgive the Green Masks. It was like being bored to death with fear. Nothing would happen for days. One morning or late evening, we are rushed out of the huts, sacks thrown over our heads. Are we going to be shot? But we are made to march and march and trip over sticks and bush. Hours and hours of it, jabbed in the back with the butt of the rifles. Finally, they take off the sacks and we go on walking and sometimes I think I will lie down and say, *Just shoot me.*

When they let us stop, we drop where we are. They shout because they want us inside the shack. We scramble in and I don't even remember lying down or closing my eyes. And the next day it will be the same. I miss Lobo.

Now, I am in this place. Caracas. Now, no one ignores me. I go to buy my newspaper, *El Nacional,* and the man wants to talk. *All right then?* Or *What song is that?* I carry my radio with me at all times. Or, *How's it going major?* He thinks I am an army person. The story was in the newspapers *Ex-marine released!* But I am not an ex-marine. They would have beaten me and shot me like they did with that other poor bastard. They said he was an American. None of us slept during the beatings. None of us ate, except for Nicon and he would eat if his own mother was killed in front of him. I hated God for what he let them do. Elsa, she was still with us then, said we shouldn't hate anyone.

While the beating was going on, the young Green Mask broke in among us and began hitting us with his gun and then wept. Said we should not judge. I didn't care about judging. I just wanted them to stop so I could sleep. Elsa

103

sat with him, the green mask. His head jammed between his knees, sobbing. She said *ssshhh, ssshhh*.

It was his gun that shot her in the end. I wonder if he thinks about that, Elsa saying *sshh sshh*, not realizing that she will receive a bullet from that sobbing bundle.

Look up at that bright city sun, that sun you can always count on to shine down onto these Caracas streets. I used to dream about this: my fantasy of one day walking along a street with no gun jammed in my back, with my arms loose and free instead of tied behind with wet, nylon cord. And I walk sometimes with a bag hanging from one hand. No one snatches it away. No one stands too close and breathes into my face. No one spits so hard it stings my eyes. Even so, I don't make eye contact with people. Some habits are hard to break.

I like the city. There are almost no trees here. If I had my way, I would cut down all the ones in the middle of streets, or in pots on corners. I would burn them down to the earth. Lobo loved the earth. You should have heard the way he talked about it. Such words; eutrophication, perennial water bodies, flooding, leaching. Those sounds are relaxing. You can say *soil bulk density* and let that phrase sit in your ear, turning over and over, the initial consonants, *s*, *b*, and the weighted *d*, leading you downwards into sleep. That's what he did. Lobo gave us the gift of sleep.

Words about the earth feel darker, quieter, than other words. Computer words, like *upload, search, toggle*, are full of small aggressive movement. You can feel them rushing to push at things, tugging information here and there. I prefer the calm whisper of pen against paper, or the firm clack of typewriter keys against paper. I am a poor typist but I enjoy the pleasure of seeking letters out, building them into words and raising the anticipation from *can* to *cane* and, in a mischievous back-flourish, *chicanery*.

Here is the man with the green scarf again; his step interrupted with a twist. He half-bows to the left from some old injury. Each morning I see him. When I leave the building, I walk between blocks in convoluted paths, circling and even retracing my steps. I long to find a path that does not intersect with anyone I recognize. And yet I see him. His scarf is not the kind of they wore in the jungle, but even so, it is pulled up over his mouth and covers half his face. It is the middle of summer. Of course, I tell myself, he is not a kidnapper. But sometimes he glances towards me, as though he will say something. I quickly turn my shoulder away so that his eyes cannot find me. I keep pepper spray and a whistle on me at all times.

But this man can't be one of them. He comes at the same time each day, tilting to one side and twisting as though he has forgotten something and wants to go back to fetch it, his green scarf slipping. Perhaps he has some horrible deformity that he struggles to hide. I, too, struggle as I shave each day. Such prominent eyes, and my face bones stick out like they are running ahead of me to accuse the whole world, *Where were you when.* My face embarrasses me. It has too much in it. I want a quiet face. I want to tell people that I don't feel excited or angry or afraid. I don't feel anything, really.

There are spiders in the sink. I leave them alone. Surely there are here for a purpose. That's what Lobo would say. Lobo loved the small creatures of the soil. Each day I watch the spiders, unwilling to turn on the faucet. There are silken threads around the taps and these will spread to the two blue mugs on the draining board. One morning I will wake up to find the whole kitchen spun tight. I can't have that. I remove the threads around the taps. The spiders must learn to stay in the sink.

I keep the radio on all night. I have a small one I can carry with me. The apartment manager calls me Radiohead. The skater-boys whoop and make circles around me as I walk. But I am listening for the faint sounds that fade in and out from where I think Bogotá is. Sometimes I hear a whole word. Sometimes it's just hiss. But even that soft noise tells me that somewhere out there is *Voces del Secuestro*, and somewhere someone's name is called and someone remembers they are alive. *We know you are there. We, too, are here and we wait for you.*

We were moved to another place. I was expecting it so I wasn't nervous when the Green Mask stood at the door of the hut and motioned with his gun. The walking did us good. We had something to endure. We were moving somewhere, even if it all seemed the same. We were moving so we knew we were alive.

When we stopped, they made us erect huts. We each had a hut. It was different from being herded into one small place; we were almost joyful at the prospect of space, privacy. We worked long after it was dark. There was a separate toilet hut and shower hut. None of us dared to think those were for us, but in the morning, they pushed us towards the huts. And that's when the relief rose up and died at the same time.

Radio Radio

We were not to be marched off at a moment's notice, but we were also here to stay.

Nicon took an old scouring pad from outside the kitchen. He carefully unraveled it and twisted the strands into a long wire. He attached it to his radio, wrapped the other end with a stone and threw it up into the dense tree-roof. It didn't fall back down. It was like watching someone throw all our dreams up to the ceiling. Then we waited until night. That's when I heard *Voces del Secuestro* for the first time. Lobo, Elsa, and me, we were astonished. Even Nicon stood up and said,

—Eehh! Can you hear that?

So now we knew. Not just we few in this part of the jungle, but all over Colombia. Everywhere there was jungle, there were the kidnapped. And from everywhere these women and their children sent messages. *We are all fine. Your daughter ran a mile in under ten minutes. We fixed the hole in the wall. Can you hear him crying? This is your new son. We love you. Don't give up. We are waiting for you.*

We were in church; sat with our heads down, not wanting the others to see the tears. I cried over and over at the same stories: the children who were going to cook their father's favorite dinner when he came back, the wife who was using her bonus to fix the boiler for hot water. I learned how to listen beneath the story-lines, to hear the hesitations that said the wife was giving up hope, that she'd met someone else, that she didn't forgive him for cheating on her, that the kids were in gangs, that they were being evicted, that they had to move in with relatives, that they had no relatives to move in with.

They spent the whole night at the radio station for a chance to talk to us. You could hear the clothes they'd dressed in. You could hear them coaching one another to speak louder, more slowly. You could hear the hope as they repeated our names, to impress on us that we were here. Some of us simply repeated the word *love* over and over, reaching to softly touch the radio. When it was her turn, Elsa kissed the radio even though Nicon had been clutching it in his dirty hands.

It was my mother who first spoke my name on the program. Six-thirty in the morning and we had listened all night to the names and the messages. She said my name as a question: *Dilan?* And my heart stood up and beat at the door of my chest. Then she said it again, firmly. *Dilan. I am waiting for you. I have painted your room blue and taken down all those old rock star posters. It's time you put up something decent. I suggest Doris Raecke. Remember that exhibition we saw?*

I hadn't talked to my mother in eight years while I'd been traveling: North America, Sweden, Australia, places of white light and soft food that vanished as soon as you bit into it. Nothing like my mother's wide plates of thick brown meat and plantains and oranges, meant to weight you to the earth, so you could never leave.

But I didn't want to be a cattle breeder or a pathologist, nor a doctor or preacher, and definitely not a coffee plantation supervisor like my father whose evenings at the plantation grew strange shadows behind the shelling machine, the women backed up against the wall, their overalls around their feet, my father's pale, knotty legs straining and shaking.

Other wives raised thin voices, threw cheap ornaments

and wooden trays. Other wives packed a bag, linked their children's hands together, stood at bus stops, chins lifted. My mother turned to her stove, asked if I'd seen the new Gonzalo Ariza exhibition, *those beautiful trees,* placed a postcard of "Mist in the afternoon" on the wall above the spice-rack. Never flinched when my father said he was moving in with the rich German woman; never spoke a word, three years later, when he moved back after the German woman threw him out. The cancer was already threading into his bones.

I was 17. I wanted to know why she stood aside and let him walk back in. I wanted to know how she could share the house with him and his fingerprints of German küchen. But she said nothing, stirred the stew while he lay on the sofa calling for thicker pillows and softer blankets.

I took the scholarship to North America and traveled steady years away from their misery. I sent no postcard, birthday card, Christmas card. I wandered the streets on holidays, looking into store windows as though doing last-minute shopping. I had no beginning, no evidence other than plane ticket stubs that had arrived from anywhere. Over the years I fell into other names: Declan, Diego, Dwayne, names that drained me away. Eventually, I slipped sideways, back into Colombia, to Cali, south of Bogatá, and taught the colors of music to blind children.

This was before I was pushed from behind, folded over and thrown into a van to lie on the floor, leaking thin streams of fear and piss.

And into this empty bottle my mother poured her voice while I crouched in the black forest night air, everyone's breath around me. She talked about my childhood, the neighbors, the parties. Her voice, crackling and low-pitched on the radio, was a voice that owned a house with electric light and curtains and a sofa with cushions. She made me look good. I felt such a rush of love for her. I longed for more of her memories so I could become the child she'd known.

I became part of the nightly human body sculpture holding up the radio, turning it this way and that for the best reception. Sometimes we held agonized positions for hours, straining our ears to hear the voices coming to us from Bogotá. When I finally heard her voice again over a month later, I almost dropped to the earth with gratitude, my heart jumping, my legs shaking. How I loved her for her belief that I was still here.

It happened to all of us as we waited; that jump of the heart, that loud beating that almost drowned out the plaintive scratchy voice. We strained to feel the breath from the mouths.

She knew, my mother, when I was released. I was marched, alone, even further than I had been before. I thought I should have at least had the chance to say goodbye to Nicon. But I was put into a plane and I thought they were going to throw me out. That's what they do with some of the kidnapped. But one of the guards whispered I was going home. The family trustee had paid the ransom. I didn't believe him until we touched down at the airport, until I stood outside on the tarmac, until uniformed men came towards me and took me into the terminal, until I had a shave and I wore new shoes and they gave me fifty dollars. I placed a call to the family trustee and thanked him. He said I should thank my mother.

Radio Radio

I should have gone to see her. I did wonder what it would be like to return to Bogotá, to the blue room with village scenes by Raecke, who wasn't even a Venezuelan artist. After all, my mother was now my only family. But when they asked me where I'd like to go, I said *Caracas*.

I didn't know how to handle all that radio love. It was easy to cry in the jungle, but at the airport I wanted to be somewhere else. I didn't know how long it would be before my gratitude would over-ripen. Maybe she'd start blaming me for my father's sorrow again. If only I hadn't left. If only I'd come home. If I'd made the attempt to travel endless miles through endless green, endless brown, over endless pot-holed roads in trucks and taxis with endless punctures. If I'd only said I'd loved him. Perhaps I didn't love him enough. What is enough? Does the love for a kidnapped child substitute for the love for a husband? And had she always loved me this sudden, quick way of the voice melting into the microphone?

I flew to Caracas, Venezuela, nestled just above Colombia's ear. I didn't look out of the window the whole way. Vertigo of the heart. Cowardice of the bowels. Nicon was still down there somewhere.

When I raise my glass, I salute Nicon who lost so much weight that we had to drop the "Fat" from his name. Nicon, whose foul language so upset Lobo that he would walk away. But Nicon kept the radio alive when it failed. Nicon stole another wire scouring pad when the wire aerial broke. In the end, you had to admire him.

When I raise my glass sometimes I forget the wine inside. The glass is so clean. It shines like Nicon's gold-plated tooth. I wonder if I should get one to honor him, but I am afraid of the dentist and a gold tooth is expensive.

I miss them, Lobo, Elsa Nicon, and the little guard who sometimes whispered things to us that he wasn't meant to; the bickering that went on, the confusion over what they really wanted. I even miss the bully-guard who beat Lobo because Lobo was easy to bully. The bully-guard's radio was nicer than ours. Once he found classical music, someone singing opera. I didn't think I liked opera, but we all stood still listening to the woman's voice lifting and falling like golden tissue. And when the bully-guard looked up and found us there he didn't yell. His eyes were wide, astonished with tears.

I raise my glass to all of them. I keep wondering if Nicon is still there or if someone came up with his ransom. I imagine him listening to the radio for someone to call his name. I thought of calling in to *Voces del Secuestro,* myself.

And I wonder how long it was before my mother gave up waiting for me to arrive home, and finally went back to *Voces del Secuestro*. Three days ago I heard her voice and I crouched on the floor, mouth open, saliva dripping onto the carpet. And with the question in her voice, *Dilan?* Everything left: the bedroom wall with the water stains, the spiders spinning fractal dreams in the sink, my new shoes, my library card, my black Pilot pen. Everything released from me, spinning orbitals around my small, pointless, cluttered planet. And I was back, fingers clenching the dirt floor, unwashed, unshaven, torn shirt and pants while my mother's voice said that she had painted my room blue, that she would keep it clean and empty for me.

Borderland

She shifts the sleeping child on her back. She has been walking for a long time across this land with no houses and no trees, no telegraph wires to indicate other human voices in the air. The road swims up against the horizon.

It is almost night. To one side she can make out a clump of bushes far from the road. Her back is burning from the weight of the child, Ticho. She must rest so she can carry him again tomorrow, so that her body will produce the milk he needs.

She steps off the road and walks across the dirt and she tries not to stumble, not to awaken the child. For a while there is nothing but the sound of her breathing and the movement of her feet crumbling dry clods of earth.

The bushes have no leaves but they are thick and thorny. There is a small space in the center of the bushes. She sets Ticho down and works quickly. Even the twigs are tough and the thorns gouge her hands. She fashions a small tunnel so she can crawl in, pulling Ticho after her on his blanket. She blocks the tunnel with the broken off twigs. Above, the last faint light from the sky and a single faint star pierce the branches weaving like wire above.

She is now still for the first time since the train blew up. She and Ticho had boarded the train—was it two or three days ago? Did they sleep on the train? Perhaps the explosion has blown a hole in her memory. She knows she was coming to meet her husband, Israel, on the border.

She was holding his letter when the train rocked sideways, the windows blew out, and fire exploded through the carriage. She grabbed Ticho and burrowed her way through a mad, writhing forest of elbows and knees. At some point, she was cut on the arm. At some point, she fell out of the carriage and scraped her shin. It was lucky she fell and that the pain was so bad she couldn't move.

There was the scrape and crunch of gravel as people fell near her. The gunshots moved further away. She stood up and ran towards the station building but it blew up, people falling like flaming comets. She turned and ran to the rocks, stumbling up the sliding scree. Ticho screamed into her neck. Any minute now they would see her and shoot her. But she climbed on, and the rocks became bigger until she was scrambling among boulders. She squeezed behind a boulder and crouched with Ticho shaking in her arms.

Impatient with the noise of her breathing, she listened for the shots to move closer or an explosion. Perhaps that would be best. Then Ticho would know nothing except this final last noise. It would be quick.

The gunshots were fainter. Ticho was whimpering and she realized she had left her bag on the train. There was no food or water.

He was two and had been weaned for four months. She offered him her dry nipple and he sucked. Perhaps he would sleep and then she could find food for him. He sucked for a long time and her nipple was sore. She moved him to the other side. He cried and asked for an apple. She coaxed him back to her nipple. He slept. She drowsed and wakened. Surely someone would find them. Was it better to be shot than to watch her child starve? In the cold, she held him close, and he slept and woke through the night, sucking at her dry breasts.

The unexpected happened at daybreak. She must have slept a little and woke to the suddenly familiar sensation of having her nipples plugged into a socket. Ticho drank hungrily first one side and then the other and she cried with relief. Eventually she would have to find food for herself, but the next business was to escape safely before the guns came back.

Ticho slept after his feed and she cautiously looked out from the boulder. The train was now a pile of steel and black embers. Nothing moved, as though some strange magic had dropped from the sky, scorched the earth and then disappeared.

She went back for Ticho and tied him on her back with his blanket. Scrambling down took a long time. How had she managed these huge rocks, this slippery scree? How had she climbed with this heavy child? If not for Ticho, she could have run further, faster, would have remembered her bag, would have held on to the letter and directions. At the bottom of the cliffs, she headed west. Surely it was possible to walk to the border from here.

It is still night when she wakes. She listens, but there is no scuffling, nothing to indicate that anything is approaching.

More stars are visible. Her shin is painful but the cut on her arm has stopped bleeding. She can walk and carry Ticho even though he is thirty pounds, about the weight of two bags of flour. She has carried those easily from the market. And Ticho must be carried.

Israel wrote that he would wait by the windmill next to a river. But this meeting place depended on her getting to the station. And the letter is gone. And she remembers that she must find food for herself so that she can continue to produce milk for Ticho.

But for now she can do nothing about any of these problems, so she examines the stars until she sleeps again.

She is wakened by the morning light, pink and blue streaked. She crawls out, careful not to disturb Ticho. There are no birds, not even crows. She stares at the sky curving towards the earth. Far away she can see a tiny pinprick of light. A house? A building? Even a single street lamp would be welcome. If there is one street lamp, there must be more and they will lead her to other people. She can ask them how to find the windmill and the river.

She rouses Ticho and feeds him. He is still half-sleeping as she eases him on to her back and ties the blanket around him securely. She reaches the roadside quickly and dismisses the burning in her stomach. As soon as she reaches the light she will find food.

All she must do is put one foot in front of the other. She is glad of the thick-soled shoes even though they are hot. She remembers the sandals Israel bought her for her last birthday. Thin, pink, leather straps and a tiny curved heel. How they had laughed over them. How she had scolded him for spending too much money. How strange and delicate her feet and ankles looked, the pink leather soft as Ticho's cheek.

A thick blur of movement undulates against the bald horizon. Eventually she can tell it is moving at speed. It can run her down in its path, can annihilate her and the child without slowing down.

She first makes out the helmets, a mob of soldiers sent to mow her down. But these are not the black helmets of the train killers. She can see colors—red and blue, white and green, yellow and orange. She can see the arms and legs moving, and the wheels. They are bent low over their bikes with the shine of sweat on their arms and legs.

She steps off the road and crouches with Ticho on her back. Even though they seem neutral she doesn't wish to draw attention. The pack flies past, none of them breaking pace, none of them looking to one side as though a fugitive woman with a small child is part of the landscape. She stares after them and then returns to the road.

As she walks on, she hears the buzz of tires returning. One of the cyclists stops a little way from her. Some way beyond him the other cyclists have stopped and are staring back at her.

He speaks her language

—You're far from home. Did you see the train accident? We have just heard about it.

It wasn't an accident. But how can she say this when he, too, might harm her?

He says,

—We're doing the ultramarathon. It's a race in time, a

year. We go everywhere. It's off limits here except for our races. So we're taking a detour to see the accident.

He makes it sound like sight-seeing.

He unstraps a water-bottle from his pack and holds it out. It is half-full. She remains where she is. He puts it down on the road. He pulls out a package of three silver-wrapped rectangles,

—Food.

He puts them beside the bottle.

She says,

—Thank you.

She would like to ask him about the river and the wind-mill, but he says, "I'd better go. They don't like anyone get-ting separated. It affects the overall timing." He races away.

She picks up the bottle and opens it. She sniffs it curious-ly, tastes the water on her dry tongue. She drinks deliriously. Ticho wakens and she gives him a little, but he is more inter-ested in her milk. The water bottle has a strap so she can carry it across one shoulder. She opens a silver-wrapped bar. It is not chocolate as she thought, but a thick, stiff substance. She is pleased by having to eat slowly. The food and water will do her good and provide milk for Ticho who is busily sucking.

The tiny light is closer now and she walks with more en-ergy. How much difference a little water and food makes. Even her leg is less painful.

She counts her steps, or talks to Ticho. Once she stops so he can void his bowel. She calls herself the Ticho Express and he laughs a little. Eventually she sees that the light she is walking towards is a large piece of metal reflecting the bald sun. What is it doing here?

Borderland

Eventually, she stands next to the round, polished disc. Is it part of something else that has been destroyed? Perhaps it is meant to reflect the sun; perhaps it is a beacon for other eyes. She scans the empty sky above her.

She gazes at each of the four straight roads leading away. The one she has come from seems identical to the others. She calculates that she has come west and must go north to meet her husband.

She sings softly to Ticho as she walks. *My little bird, come to your nest, the day is over, time to rest.* The day is not over, though. The sun has passed noon and is descending into the hottest part of the day. She must find shelter soon.

Gradually, the landscape begins to change. Far from the road, large rocks stand alone or slanted against one another. They might provide good shelter.

She is about to strike off the road and aim towards the rocks when she sees a figure running towards her. It stumbles and holds its hands out to her. Surely it means no harm, and she is even pleased to see another person.

It is a man; thin, tall, with a beard that starts and stops around his face as though negotiating a difficult problem. He is red and sweating by the time he reaches her.

He speaks her language,

—I'm so glad I caught you.

She doesn't like the word *caught* but waits to see what he will say next. He sees her water bottle,

—Give me water.

She hands it to him. He drinks deeply and then holds on to it.

She asks

—May I have it back?

—Let me carry it for you.

She holds out her hand and he reluctantly hands the bottle back. The bottle is now less than a third full. She hopes he won't ask for more.

He grins at her. The gray-white of the bridged front teeth against the other yellow ones looks like one of the dirty billboards in her old neighborhood,

—You should vote for me.

—Why?

—I'm the best person to run this country.

She has never seen anyone so unsuitable for running a country but she doesn't want to say so. He may take her water away.

—What country is this?

He stands straight like he is going to salute,

—This is God's country. Borderland.

She is elated. She must be near the border. She wants to ask if he has seen the windmill but he continues to talk.

He speaks loudly,

—Borderland is an important country. And I'm going to run it.

She thinks of something to placate him,

—I think you will win. Is anyone else going to vote?

He clicks his tongue,

Of course I'm going to win. And then I'll improve the water quality.

She is eager to refill her bottle,

—There is water? Where?

He exposes his gray teeth,

Borderland

—If you *listen*, you'll hear what I'm going to do for this country. We must have education for our children. And we need health insurance. And we need to keep out the unsavory types.

She knows he is mad, but she can't help being drawn,

—What about food?

—Do you have any?

—No.

He is a big man. He might take all the silver bars that are tied inside her skirt. She can't share these since they represent Ticho's food, too.

—I will provide enough food for every family in Borderland. And we must have better roads.

She looks around at the rocks and bare dirt,

—How will you bring food?

He describes how each family will plant vegetables, milk their cows, harvest their crops. The surplus will be exchanged with other families for goods or services.

This is like the cooperative back home. It seems simple, but it's actually a complex idea like the mad idea this man has for ruling the desert. Even if he can provide food, what is the generic gauge for *enough*?

But he believes in his simplistic ideas. She doesn't know how to leave without offending him. He may not let her go since he knows she has water.

She begins slowly moving back towards the road. He accompanies her, speaking about the need to upgrade the road. She sees a large slumping of boulders not far from the road.

She says

—We will stay here. We are used to being alone.

He shrugs,

—It's dangerous. Don't say I didn't warn you.

She slips between the rocks and climbs on until she finds a small cave where they will be safe from the president or any other predator. She settles Ticho, listening for the chattering of small pebbles that might announce the president's approach. She leans against the rock and drinks a little water. Ticho sleeps uneasily, wakes again and she nurses him to sleep. If Ticho cannot sleep what will happen? She looks at him. The still baby face, the round arms and legs. If only he weren't so heavy.

She waits while the night drags itself along. Towards morning she sleeps and it is mid-morning when she wakes. She feeds Ticho, ties him on her back and clambers down out of her cave.

As she walks towards the road, she hears the president shout. He waves at her. He must have slept close by.

She shakes her head at him and continues walking, but he runs after her. She plods on. He is a man who cannot accept or even recognize rejection,

—Don't leave. This is a good place for us. I'll make it safe.

She remembers the train, the black helmets, the white uniforms. Only soldiers could have fired so methodically at the fat man who opened his arms to beg for mercy, at the three children climbing over the tracks, at the screaming woman on her knees beside her husband.

—I must find the border.

The president wrinkles his nose as though she has said something distasteful. He follows her slowly.

Borderland

It is almost noon. The president still lags behind. She doesn't know if he is tired or secretly eating, or whether he is waiting for an opportunity to steal her water and food.

The president calls,

—We will rest here.

She keeps walking.

He calls again,

—You must stop with me.

If she doesn't stop he may be angry and she only has energy to walk and carry Ticho.

She sits to feed Ticho, her back to the president. He has moved away from them and also has his back turned. She knows he is eating and quickly unwraps part of a bar and chews, bending over Ticho so that the president can't see. She manages to drink a little water and puts the bottle away as Ticho finishes his feed.

The president walks over, scuffing the soil with his boots,

—Give me some water. You are my wife, and husbands and wives share things.

—I am not your wife.

—I want the bottle.

If she hands over the bottle he will keep it. His hand is long and the palm is a dark map. His fingernails are black-rimmed and broken. Even if his hands were clean she would not trust him.

He steps closer,

—You would let me die of thirst?

She stands up,

—What about your plans for the community?

Intent on the bottle, he is startled,

—What plans?

She is angry,

—How people would farm and grow vegetables and milk their cows. Why don't you find a cow? I would like fresh milk.

—You have fresh milk.

He grabs at her dress. It tears. Ticho, holding onto her legs, screams and the president slaps him aside. She pulls out the bottle and hits the president across the face with it,

—Take it. Leave us alone!

He snatches it and backs away,

—You hurt me.

She holds Ticho against her skin, letting him breathe her safe smell. As he cries more softly, the electric tingling of her let-down comes. She re-ties Ticho onto her back. She will feed him as soon as she can get away from the president.

It is hotter than the previous afternoon. Ticho is a wedge of lead. His hot breath blows onto her neck. She clasps her hands behind her, supporting him. She looks back. The president is crouched over her bottle. She tries to walk more quickly.

The land has lost its boulders again. One foot, the other foot, one foot, the other foot. Her shoes are cracking at the sides. How long before the seams begin to fray? How long before she will have to walk barefoot?

Ticho is asleep and hanging to one side. She shifts him so that his head is on her shoulder. What has happened to Ticho? He used to ask things and tell things but now he doesn't even say *mama*, as though the train explosion has blown

Borderland

away his words. What sense does he make of this world with no birds, no trees, no apples?

A tiny, irregular shape pushes at the horizon. The irregularities become tiny arms and she feels a surge of happiness. The windmill grows solidly in front of her, with its beautiful sails spreading.

They are less than a mile away when she makes out the fence, the endless row of white poles and the strands of wire. The windmill stands beyond.

Over the silent air comes a high-pitched hum. Ticho wakes and begins to cry. She hushes him. She slows down when she is a hundred yards from the fence. The fence is high and the deadly music is carried on a stave of thick wires running taut between the fence posts. Every Good Boy Deserves Fruit. How long since she has been able to give Ticho an apple?

There is almost enough space between the wires to push Ticho through, but not quite. Opposite the windmill there is a spot where the two lowest wires have been cut or broken. There has been an attempt to fix them, but they still sag.

She retreats, sits with her back to the fence and tries to feed Ticho. He is fretful. She moves further back until the hum is still faintly audible, but Ticho can feed. He sleeps with his hands still clutching at his ears. She knows he will waken if she tries to approach the border again.

It is almost sunset. She has nowhere to sleep except out in the open. And how will she cross the border? She cannot force a struggling two-year-old through a high-voltage fence, even if the gap is large enough. She eases Ticho off her lap and folds the blanket around him.

125

Perhaps Israel can already see her and doesn't understand why she has backed away. Perhaps he will guess that Ticho is afraid.

She starts walking towards the fence and looks back. The blanketed bundle is still. Ticho will be safe for a moment.

She reaches the fence,

—Israel!

Above the fence she strains to hear something,

—Israel! We are here! I must get Ticho.

Suddenly, Israel steps out from behind the windmill. He is thin and his clothes are shredded as though some giant hand has clawed him.

—Marta.

There is such stillness around them while the air hums the fence's song. She sees his eyes change; he cries out and she turns. Four figures are running.

The president is just ahead of three soldiers and they are all running towards the child. As Marta also runs she knows the president will reach the child before she does. A soldier drops to one knee and fires. The president falls almost on top of Ticho. The second soldier aims at Ticho. The third pushes the second away. The first runs up and tries to separate the two.

Marta, screaming, knows Ticho is also screaming. A crack and blaze as the second soldier shoots the third in the arm. The arm falls off. The first soldier aims at the second and they exchange fire. Both fall. Their guns, like tiny toys, glint golden in the last of the sun.

Marta snatches up the screaming child. There is no time to tie Ticho onto her back. Israel must find some way to get them across.

Borderland

The president has a smoking crater in his back. One of the soldiers is wounded and trying to stand. Marta grabs one of the shiny weapons and points it while the soldier tugs its black helmet off. A woman. She has thick, dark hair, like Marta. Her eyes are golden. She is weeping and says something in her language.

Marta continues to back away,

—I will shoot you.

—Gun not fire. Code lock.

The wounded woman's voice is weak. She speaks Marta's language with difficulty,

—I help you cross. Please. Water.

Marta stops. She must give the woman some water. Her arm has been shot off near the elbow,

—If I give you water, you will help us?

—Yes.

Marta finds her water bottle in the president's jacket and gives it to the wounded woman who looks at Ticho,

—So beautiful. I had child.

She drinks.

Marta hesitates,

—We should clean your arm.

The wounded woman shakes her head. She directs Marta to cut material from one of the other soldiers' uniforms. She pulls a knife from her belt. The material is thick and difficult to cut. Afterwards, Marta tucks the knife in her dress. She helps the wounded woman bind what is left of her arm, the wound is red and black, almost cauterized. The bitter smell of burning.

The wounded woman says,

—My name Telik. Come. We take him

Marta steps over to the soldier who shot at Telik. Telik shakes her head,

—We take husband.

I'm sorry is inadequate. Telik shows no emotion as she stands over her dead husband. Marta ties Ticho on her back while Telik slips her helmet strap over her husband's leg and lifts it.

Marta doesn't understand what Telik is doing but they are doing something together. She lifts the other leg and they begin pulling the body towards the fence. The body catches on everything.

Marta asks,

—How will you get back?

Telik shakes her head,

—They give order. Fence break. We go find one man.

She jerks her head back towards the other soldier,

—She want kill you child. I stop her. She go kill me. My husband shoot her.

Marta is trembling. This woman saved Ticho. The smell of burning pushes down her throat. As the hum from the wires increases, Ticho cries and kicks frantically in his blanket, and Marta and Telik stumble, imbalanced, struggling to keep moving. Telik motions for them to stop. She breathes hard. She nods and they begin pulling again, the body gathering dirt, stones, broken sticks.

They drop the body next to the fence. Israel stands helplessly beyond.

Marta says,

—She will help us. She was shot.

Borderland

—What happened? Is Ticho okay?

Marta nods. Exhausted. Speech is lost in the smell and the noise of the wires.

Telik looks behind,

—They come. Soon. You go fast.

Her face is almost yellow,

—We put this. She points from her dead husband to the sagging second wire,

—Push child through. And you. But fast.

She indicates the uniform and black helmet,

—This not burn. Not con-ductor.

Already Telik's eyes are glazing over and Marta guesses that she might be close to passing out. She says,

—You come too.

—No.

Marta wants to argue, but they must go quickly. They lift the uniformed body and drop it over the lower wire. The wire sags and the body surges and begins to smoke. Ticho has vomited.

Telik pushes her,

—*Go.*

There is plenty of room to pass Ticho through, but he is terrified and clings to her. She can feel the heat from the body as she struggles with Ticho and the stench of burning flesh makes her gag.

Israel, reaching between the wires, grabs the screaming child. Telik pulls Marta back. Ticho is safe as the body melts over the wire. The uniform and helmet of Telik's husband are intact even though the body must be entirely burned.

Telik,

—You go.

Marta is weeping,

—It's too late.

Telik lifts her hand and wipes Marta's face,

—You *go*.

Her voice is quiet; perhaps it is because she is injured. She points to Israel clutching their son.

—Go *fast*.

Marta understands and her tears come faster. She kisses Telik's hand and looks into the golden eyes.

Telik puts on her helmet, fumbling at the clasp until Marta, dry sobbing, holds it in place for her. Telik drops on top of the remains of her husband's suit, and the hissing surges again along with the stench of burnt flesh. Marta forces herself to swallow the smell as Israel's strong hands jerk her through. She doesn't touch Telik's melting backbone and shoulders, the soft fall of hair that must already be shriveled. As Marta's feet pass through, scorched with the heat, one of her shoes falls off and withers on the wire.

The hissing dies away. Israel picks up Ticho and pulls Marta after him. The soldiers will come. She kicks off the other shoe and runs beside Israel.

The tree-shadows lift their arms. She hears the strange rushing sound of water. Israel takes them further into the forest. He makes a shelter from branches and coaxes the child inside. She feeds Ticho and he sleeps. What will he remember of all of this?

She wakes to find she is holding on to Israel's hair.

He says,

—It's safe. They cannot cross the border.

Borderland

But how does he know? He talks about meeting friends in the next valley. Her world has been flat, barren, dry. She is unused to speaking of valleys and forests, trees and rivers.

His friends will help them find their new home. She is happy because he is with her and Ticho again. But who else can she trust? She thinks: *Be at peace* for her friend who is dead, whose smoking bones hang in the night air, who loved her husband and, for a moment, Ticho. What would it take to lie across an electric wire so that someone else might be free? Marta knows she could not.

She looks up and sees the night sky between the leaves. For now she can do nothing about any of these problems, so she examines the stars until she sleeps again.

A Nigerian In Paris

The pigeons own Paris. They waddle around Gare du Nord, neatly dodge the pimps and rogue taxi drivers, head straight for the Hagen Daaz tables to peck between the backpacks and suitcases on wheels.

Outside the station, taxis peel off with clumps of tourists. Women in short skirts attempt to jump the line and are sent back to stand among the pigeons, who duck and bob for crumbs attached to wedges and spikes and platforms and sneakers and suede boots with peep toes. And everywhere is the tumbril rumbling of small suitcase wheels that judder and panic and twist and overturn their burdens over the pretentious, archaic, necessary cobblestones.

The boys from Senegal, Nigeria, Mali, the Congo, thin arms and legs that don't fill the blue check shirts and beige pants, sidle up on worn Puma sneakers. *Your taxi hasn't arrived? I can help you.* Their accents are French. The tourists avert their eyes.

The pigeons peck relentlessly between the feet of black and white and brown. They peck at the ground, backpacks, suitcases, shoes; crumbs from a sandwich, chicken nuggets, paper smeared with ketchup. They peck among themselves, at a weaker pigeon, at the breast feathers of a sodden corpse.

Packs of station police in tight black shirts and baggy pants slink back and forth, semi-automatic guns slung over their shoulders, pale hands across black barrels. No one asks them for directions. The pigeons and the unofficial taxi drivers stick to the shadows.

Neatly threading his way between them, the Nigerian is on his way to his night watchman shift. Despite the mild September night, he wears a heavy coat to bulk up his slight frame. The fedora is pulled down to hide the narrowed eyes, thin eyebrows. Just visible: the short nose and cupid-bow mouth. He walks slightly slower than city pace. The gentle stride masks the limp in his right leg; an old unevenly-healed femoral fracture.

The lights shine along the wide boulevards where the beggars are part of the romantic sights. Mostly women, they are dressed in shawls and long dresses; their heads partly covered. They kneel on the wide boulevards, motionless. Their heads are bowed. They press their hands together. They do not look up. They look like the carved figures in churches and cathedrals, the stone intermediaries who convey monied petitions. They pray among the waddling pigeons and tourists. There is no food to be gleaned. A few coins sit in old McDonald's paper cups.

The Nigerian arrives at the Julien Patisserie off Rue D'Alsace, checks around the premises and settles himself at the first of several posts between which he will rotate during the night. During his four months on the job, only one confrontation. Two guys, laughing, drunk, calling *Eh, noiraud, viens ici.* And then they came at him, swinging a cricket bat. Sudden tightening at the back of the throat; sudden taste of salt-adrenaline and he moved without thinking. And then:

Jèsu, mon bras! C'est cassé!

He broke your arm? Nom de dieu. . . .

Regard moi. Je t'emmerde! You are crazy, you know?

On y va. Putain.

You should be locked up. Vas te faire foutre. . . .

It is three-thirty when his final shift is over. He returns to the patisserie where the baker's assistant gives him day-old bread: a baguette and three brioches. The Nigerian walks to a small park off the Quai de Valmy to eat his breakfast, to sleep on a bench. If it rains there is a large oak tree for shelter. If the rain is very heavy it is better to walk.

And he walks through his own red wound as he travels the boulevards and the avenues and the streets where the store windows reflect his mother's face, the faces of his sisters, his father, over and over until the dawn grows enough to hide them and all he can see is his own faceless reflection. It is better not to see and yet he longs for them. It is hard to think of that time but it exists: his father's long arms lifting thatch to repair the roof, his mother's quiet song as she moved around the hut in the evenings, his sisters teaching him the hand-clapping game. This was First World before the Knife-Men came and made everything red.

From the taxi drivers at Gare du Nord he hears the talk about the Christians. The homeless, the refugees spread themselves out, a few at this church, two or three at another. How kind the Christians are. They give you food. They give you clothes that are terrible, but they are warm. Sometimes you can find shoes. The Adventists give even more than others, he hears. He starts attending the Wednesday evening prayer meetings at the Adventist church near the Lanboisiére Hospital, not far from the Gare du Nord station.

Within a week, he has clothes and food that he can carry in his satchel. He is still sleeping on the bench in the park but he doesn't say anything, unwilling to believe that his luck will hold. Who would give a bed to someone like him?

After a month, a woman from the church leaves a message for him. He cannot stay outside in all weathers. He must stay with her family. He understands her need to do good. He, too, comes from dark needs that he can't explain.

She and her family are Mauritians. They live in the *banlieue*, where the working people live. They have money but not much. The Nigerian is familiar with Christians and poverty from his own country. Rich people don't need Christianity.

Her husband is a tall man who drives a taxi. The husband collects the Nigerian from his park bench. As they drive, the husband talks about everything they pass. *This is Orly airport. There is another airport further north called Charles de Gaulle. This is the banlieue but we call it the countryside. It is very quiet here. Here is the station where the train runs into Paris. It is expensive. We don't take the train often.*

The husband explains that they don't have a house, only an apartment. The Nigerian understands. This is not where you find the luxuries of Lagos: thick carpets and air conditioning. Even so, he is to sleep inside and this is a luxury. He is curious to see what it will be like after these months of living outdoors and fighting off razor-colored dreams from

A Nigerian In Paris

Second World. Perhaps the dreams can be locked out as easily as you lock a front door.

The Nigerian walks into the apartment and inhales their lives: the perfumes of rice and chicken and chocolate bread and kiwi fruit and oranges and berries, and scent and makeup and the pretty, cheap clothes of the young. Two young daughters aged ten and fifteen in school uniforms. The young one has a row of silver and red barrettes threaded into her hair, pulled back in two short lop-sided bunches. The older girl has a blue ribbon neatly tied at the end of her long braid. Out of respect, out of fear, he doesn't make eye contact with them, and only briefly meets the wife's eyes during their introductions.

He is to share their home: one living/dining room, one kitchen, two small bedrooms, one toilet, one shower. He imagines how they flow through this space between the small rooms. He must also learn to do this. By the front door, the neat row of shoes; flip-flops, tennis shoes, high-heeled pumps and a small pair of flowered rain boots. He will hand them the shoes that will carry them along paths that mark their days, finally coming back to this place near the door. Shoes are important. He has filed a slot in the heel of his right shoe where he keeps his knife.

They show him how the shower works, where he must put his clothes so they can be washed in the heavy duty cleaning cycle. They will clear a place for him to sleep in their living-and-dining room. The parents are out during the day. The husband takes the older daughter to her all-girls school in his taxi and she comes home on the school bus. The wife walks the young one to and from the local primary school.

The Nigerian will be left alone in the house to sleep. He will be gone to his job before they come home. They are so trusting.

The husband sits on the sofa with a large suitcase opened in front of him. By his side is a huge drying frame where small towels hang like pennants. There must be at least fifty of them. *They are from the church*, the husband explains, *for the foot-washing*. What foot-washing has to do with church is beyond the Nigerian but he watches as each towel is folded into three and then placed lengthwise in the suitcase. The suitcase can take three towels per row. Back and forth across the rows, each carefully folded towel is pressed into place while the husband talks about never wearing shoes until he was a teenager. *Back in Mauritius I didn't need shoes. These Paris fashion shoes are so narrow that they can cut your feet in half. Me, I can only wear baskets.*

There is something holy about the way the husband folds each towel and places it into the suitcase as though he is delivering blessings. The Nigerian man is mesmerized, follows each fold, each placement, each gentle touch of the fingers. The husband finishes his folding and sets the table for dinner; each placemat, each knife and fork, each napkin. There are no rough or sudden movements. The Nigerian man waits. Even a gentle person has their limits.

At dinner, there is laughter and the two girls compete for their parents' attention and affection. He, too, is included in their discussions. The young girl asks: *Do you wear sandals or flip flops? Is the summer hotter or colder than here? Do you like opera or rap?*

The older girl shakes her head. *Don't ask so many questions.*

A Nigerian In Paris

She smiles, her eyes looking directly into his. Her eyes remind him of his sister's. In fact, all of them are like his own family from First World. How can he stay here?

But he can hear the driving rain against the windows. If he leaves now where can he shelter for the night? He glances at the wife's face. It is shining with good will. She nudges the bowl of potatoes toward him,

—So you must be invited to take more?

—Thank you.

Nibbles at the potatoes. A stone where his stomach should be. He is hungry. He needs to eat. But he can't swallow the food, can barely finish what is on his plate.

—It was delicious. You are a fine cook. I am very grateful.

But his stomach burns with some flame that he cannot understand.

The girls clear the table and their father washes the dishes while they wipe and put everything away in a great clashing of crockery and silverware. They shout with laughter as their father beats a rhythm on one of the pots. The younger girl begins a song; sweet-strong, pineapple juice voice and the older one adds a soft counterpoint. Instantly, the Nigerian remembers his own sisters singing in the close harmony that he has rarely heard since leaving home.

He remembers the other sounds they made. Even their screaming was not as harsh as the screams he heard from others in Second World. With those ones it was better to kill them quickly before the screaming got into his brain. At first he stuffed balls of cotton into his ears. Once, when someone fired a gun too near him, he lost most of the hearing in his right ear. Afterwards he didn't have to use nearly as much cotton.

The wife comes back in and sits down at the table with him,

—Come. Let's move this table so we can make your bed.

He gets up and obediently helps her move the table and chairs, carry the mattress in and cover it with pink and green striped sheets, even though these are the tasks of a woman. They are beautiful, these sheets. He has never seen anything like them. There is a small band of green satin around one end, about a foot from the top, so you can tell which end should be placed where the pillow will go. He likes this sense of orderliness. He likes how he and the wife shake out the sheets and tuck them around the mattress. It reminds him of how he used to make the beds with his mother when he was small, before it was unacceptable for a boy to make beds, before the silver knives came that cut the air before they landed.

He spends a few moments tucking in the sheet at the bottom so that he can regain his balance before he stands. Sometimes the memories slip in sideways before he has a chance to close them off in a separate room. There is more than one room: one is for his family. There are other rooms for other families, or a single man or a woman who looked straight into his eyes before they died. Most of them closed their eyes. He liked it better that way, too. He feels the doors shifting on their hinges. He leans against them, locks them firmly. *Enough.*

The girls have finished their showers and the husband comes in to tell him that the bathroom is now free. The wife hands him a small, white towel and a green wash-cloth. She apologizes because they don't match but he likes these cool colors. He holds them against his face and breathes in the delicious smell of fabric softener. She hands him a new toothbrush. Dark pink, the deep color of the hibiscus outside his mother's house.

The bathroom is filled with the scents of the soaps and shampoos that the girls have used. Their wet towels are hanging on the door. They have left nothing else behind; no dirty clothes thrown on the floor, no dark finger-marks on the sink, no toothpaste half-squeezed out of the tube. They were already so clean. He would gladly cover himself with their left-over perfumed bath-water so that he might disappear into the sweet, bland, *banlieue* life.

He does not wish to use the shower. He crouches in the bathtub and pours water over himself with the plastic jug he finds next to the sink. There are so many soaps to choose from. Some, shaped like seashells, are arranged in a small basket. Others are in bottles: coconut and lime, orange and verbena, lavender and mint. One large green bar of soap sits in a curved white dish. The Nigerian guesses that this is the soap the husband uses. He, too, uses it to wash both his body and hair. He has not washed like this in a long time and turns his face up under the thread of water pouring from the jug. He opens his mouth and lets the water fill it, lets it run out over his teeth and lips. How beautiful to feel the warm water against the mouth. He swallows, feels it filling him.

Finally, he steps out of the tub and towels himself. He glances at the tub. Dark residue. He finds a scouring pad in a bucket under the sink. He kneels down and uses the green soap to clean out the tub. He watches with satisfaction as all the dirty water swirls away down the drain. The tub looks exactly like it did when he first got in. He breathes in the smell of his skin. He smells just like the bathroom. He cleans his teeth with the new toothbrush

He puts on the t-shirt and pants that the husband left for him on the toilet seat. He bundles up his dirty clothes, hardly wishing to touch them. They belong to someone else who has been washed out of the tub into the sewer system.

He drops off his clothes near the laundry basket next to the washing machine and goes back into the living room. The husband is spreading a tablecloth across the table. The wife is brushing the girls' hair. The older one is securing her long braid with a white band. She is wearing a yellow robe over her green and blue pajamas. She smiles at him and flicks the long braid back,

—Bon nuit.

The flick of the braid, the smile. He feels that she has said something to him. She kisses her mother and father and sister, and leaves the room.

The Nigerian ducks his head,

—*Bon nuit*.

The father teases the younger daughter who is complaining as her mother brushes out the tangles.

This could be his own mother brushing out his younger sister's hair while he makes faces at her to make her smile.

They cut her right through the neck, the men who came with their blind blades. He had stepped in front of his sister. *Stop*. But they pushed him aside and his sister looked up with her calm eyes and the blade came down on her, as their mother screamed, *Please, not my child*. And then the blades fell on his mother. They found every part of her body and those men breathed in and out and gasped and laughed as she died. And then someone grabbed him by the waist and he thought he was next but they bundled him out of the hut. Outside, he saw his father lying motionless with darkness all around him in wide pools. From a tree the body of a baby dangled, its head almost severed. He kicked and cried out but they held him and brought him to that place, with other boys from his village. His age-mates. But none of them could look at each other because that meant they would have to look at what had happened, the thing that had pushed the earth into the air and forced the trees to fruit blood: the birth of Second World.

Enough. He closes his eyes. For a moment the floor rises beneath him and then settles as the little girl says,

—*Ow.*

—Hold still.

—I'm going to cut *all* my hair off.

—*Bon. Finis.*

The little girl kisses the husband and wife and comes to him, holding her arms up. *Une petite bise.*

He is startled but leans down so that she can kiss first his right cheek, then the left, then the right once more. They are solid kisses and her flower-and-toothpaste-scent fills his head, pushes away the darkness.

—You smell nice now. Did you use my lavender shampoo?

—No. Just the soap.

The husband and wife smile at him, usher her out of the room. *Bonsoir, bon nuit. Dormez bien.*

The clock on the table: not even nine o'clock. Do they always sleep so early? Perhaps it is because of the children.

Perhaps it is because he is now sleeping in the only room where the husband and wife can go after the children have gone to bed. He sits on the mattress and crosses his legs. Tonight he will sleep without shoes. He stretches his toes and arches his feet.

He touches the blanket. It is rough in the woven parts and smooth at the edges where the shiny binding material has become soft. He likes it because it is old. It has come from many years before this one where he sits alone in a strange home.

He would like to see what is inside the drawers of the tall cabinet on which the husband put the suitcase full of folded towels. He wonders what small treasures the family has collected. Silver knives and forks? Carving knives? Perhaps one long carving knife for Sundays when they have their roast dinner. A carving knife can be very useful. But this family wouldn't have a strong one. Theirs would be only for chicken or roast beef. The handle has become loose with the years of washing. Sometimes, as the husband carves the chicken, the handle and the blade fall apart. The family laughs. The wife hands the husband a cloth so that he can wipe the blade and slot it back into the handle. They joke about buying a new one. They don't have money to spend on anything good. They will buy another cheap carving knife that will also fall apart in another year. Their weakness touches him. What can happen to a family whose carving knife is so fragile?

The shimmer of something silver flickers on the edge of his memory. He blinks it away, tucks his canvas bag under his pillow, slips between the sheets, pulls the blanket around him. The mattress receives him softly and he lies awake a little longer to appreciate how nothing pokes into him, nothing hurts his hip or back.

He cannot hear the outside sounds of night. No one's cart on limping wheels judders across broken pavement, with a sound like rattling cages. No cat suddenly jumps from a stone pillar near the quiet fountain. No one makes the rapid, urgent sounds of sex. No one sings, laughs, weeps, begs, cries out in pain. No one wakes suddenly, screaming. No one dies.

There is no comforting bench-back to lean against. He can't smell the cat piss or the faint smell of rosemary from a second-floor balcony. Where is everything? The walls are too close and the smell of dinner is still here, lying on the floor under the dining table. All those potatoes. Where did they go? If he reaches out, will he find one? Has the ceiling got lower since he lay down? If he stands, will he strike his head?

A sensation of falling. It almost feels like going to sleep, but the drowning sensation intensifies and he knows something is coming for him. He struggles to wake properly and confront the demon, reaches for the knife in his shoe but he is not wearing his shoes. He sits upright, flings his arms out and grasps flesh—a leg—an ankle—yanks it closer. A stumble of limbs. A long braid hits him in the face and he smells lemongrass.

The girl who flicked her braid as she said goodnight. He does not have to kill her.

She is breathing quickly.

She pushes him away with a furious whisper,

—What are you? Some kind of rapist?

—What—what is going on?

—I am getting a drink of water. If that's all right with you.

But the kitchen is a separate room, opposite the bathroom. What is she doing here? His heartbeat is still hard, fast,

—I'm sorry. I didn't realize. I hurt you?

A soft laugh,

—You're lucky it wasn't Patrice. She would have *screamed*.

—La petite?

—Not so small.

Silence.

Her shivery breath,

—Fait froid.

He sits upright, still,

—Then you must go back to bed.

—You could let me have some of the blanket.

So the husband and wife will come in to find their daughter in bed with him. He isn't afraid of the wife who will shrill at him and accuse him of being ungrateful. It is the husband, who he will have to hurt, whose eyes will follow him as he grabs his clothes, rushes away from the house into this *banlieue*. How far is it to Gare du Nord?

—It is not a good idea.

—I'll go in a minute. I want to know what it's like.

Ah, the bourgeois question. What is it like to be poor, to not know where your next meal is coming from, to live in a park, on a bench?

—What do you mean?

—To be black.

He smiles in the darkness,

146

A Nigerian In Paris

—You are also black.

—We are *Mauricienne. We* are not black.

He wants to laugh. In Paris, if you are not white, then you are black. She doesn't know this? No, she knows she is black but he is her redemption because he is blacker.

She is curious,

—But you are from *la vrai Afrique.* You have traveled. Me, I have never been anywhere.

She settles on the mattress beside him. He feels the blanket move, and the touch of her foot, her ankle. In a moment he will feel her hard body up against him. She will curl her back against his private, pretend she doesn't feel his erection, wait for his arms. He can feel *want* rising off her skin.

—Your parents—

She exhales impatiently,

—Ah. They will never wake up. I've been out of the house at night. They never knew. I was with friends. *Boys,* sometimes.

He doesn't care what she's done. If she will just go and he can make it through this night he can leave in the morning. It is safer to stay outside where the air is not blunt, unmoving.

She wriggles her foot against his shin,

—So. You have been with lots of women?

—Yes.

Strictly speaking, rape isn't sleeping with anyone, but when he took these women, girls who were younger than this one's sister, he fell into the no-time place. Surely that is a kind of sleep.

In Second World you caught the girl, bound the mouth, forced yourself between the thighs before slitting the throat.

Here in Third World, his only women are the old ones around the park who accept a stale brioche or two as payment, and sometimes they must be roughed up a little to cooperate.

She will tell her friends she was with a *real* African man. *Moi, je comprends. Tous les Africains. Ils sont come ça.* But he is not a real anything. The husband in this house is real. The wife is real. But he is splintered into three; an over-scribbled wall of color-blooded graffiti. He has one chance left, one world to make sense of and this girl is trying to trick him with her foot and her smooth leg and her movement under the blanket.

Even though he cannot see her, he can sense her warm outline. His hand against the hard outline of his right shoe beneath the pillow. The quick blade comes to his hand. She will not struggle much. No one will wake up. He can slip out without anyone hearing. This much he knows how to do.

The sudden smell of citrus. A whisper from the doorway,

—Miriam?

Hiss of breath,

—Patrice? What are you doing here?

—What are *you* doing here with the *noiraud*?

—Patrice, just go back to bed.

—I will tell Maman.

—*Merde.*

The cold shock of street language.

The citrus smell is stronger as Patrice sits down near him and wriggles closer,

—Give me some of the cover.

The two girls yank the quilt back and forth. A heel strikes his shin. These girls have hard feet. He slides the knife back into the shoe, keeps his hand on it.

148

A Nigerian In Paris

He moves, sits a little way from them on the carpet,

—Go back to bed now before your parents come in. Both of you.

He can see their outlines. Both sitting up. Both holding on to the quilt.

Patrice's whisper, full of laughter,

—Come, Miriam. We can play one game.

The Nigerian is astounded,

—A game?

—I-Spy.

Miriam,

—Are you a complete idiot? How can we play I-Spy?

He hears Patrice trying not to laugh aloud,

—I go first. I spy with my little eye, something black.

—Patrice, everything is black here. Let's go.

The smothered giggle again,

—*Non.* You must guess *first.* And I am thinking of *one* thing.

He sighs,

—It is me.

He feels her hand touch his arm,

—Yes—you guessed!

Miriam whispers authoritatively,

He is not a *thing.* And he is not so black.

He hears the whisper of their robes, their feet as they leave.

He is a black thing, a *noiraud.* He is a not-so-black thing. He is nothing and something and nothing, except for one thing he owns. His voice, small and bent, whispers to the space they have left.

Sandra Hunter

—My name is Bem.

The name given by his father. The name lost for years in the other names of *scum, rat, cockroach*. Bem,

—It means peace.

Where the Birds Are

Sadiq can make a mustache by holding a pencil under his nose and curling his upper lip. Hunri-Howri says that it's because Sadiq's nose is bigger than the backside of Mrs. Rashad's pig. Sadiq says that Hunri-Howri couldn't hold a pencil in both hands without dropping it. Side by side, they look like a comic act; Hunri-Howri nodding an overlarge head on a thin neck with an Adam's apple like an egg, Sadiq lifting his round face up to smile, cross-hatched teeth and ears like jug handles.

Two weeks ago, and despite the bomb warning, they were looking for birds' eggs by the river outside their village, high in the mountains and so far north of Dera Baba that a strong, determined gale might baseball-batter it over the snarling, snowy teeth of India into Pakistan. The eggs are a delicacy, but Farhad, who is an apprentice at the mosque, says that it is inconsiderate towards God's creatures to steal the young. Even so, Farhad eats the eggs straight from the shell.

When the bomb landed, less than a mile away, Hunri-Howri and Sadiq were standing between two trees whose smooth white roots crawled into the water. The surface of the river shimmered, like milk about to boil; then it shook, coiling and thumping the banks. Hunri-Howri, easily out-running Sadiq, shouted over his shoulder to hurry up before God smote them. Sadiq was angry that Hunri-Howri could run and shout at the same time

Sadiq's mummy cuffed them until their ears felt like liquid fire and hugged them painfully tight until they couldn't breathe. Hunri-Howri, unfamiliar with maternal affection, was too surprised to resist.

Not everyone was as lucky. The village now has three fresh mounds of earth, standing sad and red at the far side of the *masjid*. Visitors come with flowers or prayers. The old ones don't cry, but beat the ground with their sticks. The children bring leaves or stones to leave at the grave-sides of the uncle and two aunties who no longer pinch cheeks, hand out sweets or call *Namaskar*.

Sadiq's mother is chopping vegetables with a small, curving knife. He watches the silvered point as it flashes through the onion. He imagines his mother as a warrior, like some of the women he's heard about in other border villages, bravely attacking the invaders, stabbing them three, four times. They say the women don't even wipe their knives before using them. He wonders what it would be like to be stabbed by a knife smelling of onions or garlic.

His mother wipes her hands,

—Go to Mrs. Rashad and get me sugar, one packet. Buy white only. And Sadiq? Careful, now.

She puts the R10 in his hand and pushes him out of the kitchen.

Where the Birds Are

Mrs. Rashad's shop is on the corner of Pitti and Kapla where the big tree has shade enough for six chairs and a table. The old men sit there, drinking tea and smoking and calling, *Any news?* There are only five of them these days. They don't talk about Pratap except to curse him for not being in a safer place. He has made them more nervous. Which of them hasn't thought about their slow paths home?

—When the next one comes, I will just lie down. It will save the fall.

—I will jump up to meet it.

—You haven't jumped in forty years, Munir.

—It is a mistake. They never bomb this side.

—It isn't Pakistan—it's these hotheads from Iran.

—Kkkaaa. You all talk rubbish, Ruchira, bring more tea. The old ones are suffering from heatstroke.

—The prime minister has said there will be no more. So, who will win the cricket this season?

Mrs. Rashad gives him the sugar in a brown paper packet, and a handful of change,

—You go straight home, Sadiqui.

Sadiq begins running down to the river where Hunri-Howri lives. Along Kapla, the huts are more ragged, as though roofing is optional and walls don't always come in sets of four. They crowd together, lending each other support and the occasional shared wall. Beyond lies the torn party balloon of the shanties. Sadiq walks past the plastic sheeting and fluttering cotton walls and, on one of the rubbish heaps near the river, sees Hunri-Howri, a tall crow-with-no-tail.

Hunri-Howri frowns at him,
—What is it?
—Sugar.
—Rich people.
Sadiq wishes the sugar packet were not taped shut, then he could let Hunri-Howri have a little,
—How are your bruises?
—The ones on my leg? Those are nothing. Look at this.
He lifts the back of his shirt and shows Sadiq the dark brown-purple patches, like continents shifting across the rib-cage and ridged backbone.
Sadiq is impressed,
—Ka, did he beat you with a pole? Such a big lump. Does it hurt?
Hunri-Howri pulls his shirt down,
—Come on, let's go and see Farhad.
They walk back between the sagging rubbish heaps, occasionally grabbing handfuls to throw in the river or at each other. Not even the rag-pickers come here; the mounds are stringy with shorts threads of unraveled cotton, thick with rotten cardboard, a rendez-vous for crows. They skirt around the back of the shanties where an old woman calls to Hunri-Howri.
—You are not going home, son?
—Not yet, Aunty.
—You come here tonight. Amir says Dadda is staying with him for now.
—Thank you, Aunty, but I will go home.
—Son, Amir says your father is unwell. Angry and shouting and all. You should stay here for a while.

Where the Birds Are

Hunri-Howri stands very still. He looks like he's stopped breathing,

—I will bring food, Aunty.

Sadiq is stunned. He has never heard such a respectful, even gentle, tone rise from the shackles in Hunri-Howri's mouth. The old woman is not a relative. Hunri-Howri has never mentioned her before. Although her shanty is missing a cotton wall and the plastic roof is torn, Sadiq sees that the sticks supporting the shanty are firmly rooted and strongly tied. Hunri-Howri has already walked on, leaving Sadiq to mutter a greeting before catching up.

—Who's that?

—None of your business.

—Is she a relative?

Hunri-Howri pushes Sadiq angrily,

—Be quiet. And don't talk about her to anyone.

At the corner of Pitti and Kapla, old Munir sits fanning a friend who has fallen asleep. He calls to Sadiq,

—Where, now, in such a hurry?

Hunri-Howri hangs back, kicks the dirt. He walks a little way off and looks up into the wide-spreading tree,

—Home, Uncle, to bring the sugar.

—You bought the sugar an hour ago. You'll have your ears pulled. Hurry, now. Don't let the bomb catch you.

Ruchira comes out with a plate of sliced mango,

—Come, Munir, leave the child alone.

Watery eyes try to focus on the two children as they go,

—That one is trouble. Look at the father, only. Drunk every day.

Ruchira says,

—Sad, nuh? And the mother dead and all. How can a child grow up properly without a mother?

—Mothers. *Tcha.* Sadiq's mother lets her son hang around with that nomad boy.

—What, nomad? Wasn't the mother Vaishya?

—The father is Shudra. They are *Shudra.*

—Eh, Munir. Calm down. I am only joking. Here is more tea.

Sadiq's mother opens the kitchen door and lifts her chin towards the gate where Hunri-Howri is waiting,

—What is he doing here?

—Mama, he is not doing anything.

—You tell him to go home.

—He is hungry.

—Cha. You can almost see his backbone through his stomach. Bring him in here. And don't let your father know.

Sadiq brings his friend inside.

—Sit, sit.

She puts two chapatis and some vegetable curry on a plate. Hunri-Howri hesitates. She repeats,

—Sit.

She puts the plate in front of him and stands back.

Sadiq sees Hunri-Howri's hunger swallow the plate. He is unused to having anyone watch him. He looks at Sadiq, but Sadiq says,

—It's for you.

Sadiq's mother touches Hunri-Howri's shoulder. It is only reflex when he raises an arm to protect himself, but she steps backs quickly. She says,

Where the Birds Are

—Rinse the plate when you've finished. Sadiq will show you.

She goes into the house.

Hunri-Howri eats almost without breathing. He uses his fingers to wipe up the last of the curry. Sadiq says,

—That's what the chapati is for. You use the chapati and wipe the plate.

Hunri-Howri finishes cleaning the plate. He says,

—Your mother makes curry like my grandmother. She died when I was six. She had the cholera, like the others.

Sadiq shows Hunri-Howri how to turn the tap.

—I've seen that thing before.

—I know.

Hunri-Howri is angry that he ate their food. He wishes there were more. He suddenly remembers his promise to take food to Aunty and feels sick with guilt. He could have shared this food with her. How she would have enjoyed the curry. He glances at the pans on the stove. Sadiq says,

—Let's go and find Farhad. I'll tell Mamma we are going.

Sadiq goes into the house and Hunri-Howri stands alone in the kitchen with his heart-beat filling his pockets. It takes only a moment to lift the cloth over the big pan and slip a hot chapati inside his shirt.

He is wiping his hand on his shorts when Sadiq's mother comes in to say goodbye. Hunri-Howri backs to the kitchen door, stammering his thanks.

Sadiq's mother says,

—So, you can come here again for your dinner.

He half bows and the chapati burns his chest.

—What is wrong?

Hunri-Howri shakes his head. Sadiq's mother shakes hers. He backs out of the door, Sadiq following with big-big eyes.

As they walk, Hunri-Howri removes the chapati from his shirt,

—I need something to wrap this in.

Sadiq's eyes are like a baby monkey's.

—You took a chapati from my mother?

Hunri-Howri says nothing.

—If you ask my mother, she will give you curry also to take to your Aunty, and even a bowl to take it in.

—You think you're so high up because you have a tap for water and chairs at the table and a colored shade on the light.

—You stole from us.

—I didn't steal. Your mother gave me the food.

—She didn't give you *this* food.

Sadiq pushes Hunri-Howri and the chapati falls to the ground. He picks it up and returns it to his shirt.

Sadiq watches Hunri-Howri walk away quickly. He remembers the six rupees in his pocket that he should have returned to his mother. He catches up with Hunri-Howri and shows him the coins,

—Let's get jellabies.

—Did you steal it?

—It's my money.

Hunri-Howri pulls his funny half-grin at Sadiq,

—You'll get in trouble.

Sadiq's hand is open, the coins on his palm. Hunri-Howri could snatch them and run off, but he does something strange. He closes Sadiq's hand over the money,

Where the Birds Are

—I don't want jellabies.

Sadiq doesn't believe him. He's joking around. In a moment, he'll start squeezing Sadiq's hand so that the coins will drop out.

Sadiq says,

—Farhad says Bhopul has something he keeps a secret even from the imam.

Hunri-Howri shrugs but lets Sadiq pull him along.

They walk along Sena Street and slow down to make the most of the smells from the restaurants and roast meat stalls. They see Bhopul eating roast chicken and talking with Lassi Man,

—I am telling you. One time. Bang. All gone.

Lassi Man wobbles his head and wipes his metal pitcher,

—Arré, baba. Go'rnment will stop them.

—Did they stop the last one? Hah? One bang. That's all.

They turn at the bottom of Straight Street past the *masjid*, a small, white square building. The clouds swim down over the mountains. Looking back, Sadiq can't even see the trees at the end of Straight Street. The village must be invisible. The *muezzin*, a cheerful old man with bad breath, will surely have a damp beard this evening. The mist makes a halo around Hunri-Howri's hair. For a moment he looks like someone in a movie, someone about to do something desperate or brave. Starlings are fighting in the gutter. They peck at each other mercilessly; one has a tuft of feathers missing above one eye. Hunri-Howri kicks at them and they fly off, swearing.

Behind the *masjid*, the two boys follow a long path through the wet grass to a tiny hut, once used for storing wood. Farhad comes out, blinking against the light, his fingers blotched and black.

—Eh, Farhad. You are writing?

Sadiq says *writing* casually, as though it is something everyone does.

—I have to do two pages today. I already made a mistake and Bhopul beat me.

—Bhopul is an old woman. He can barely lift the stick. Listen, show us Bhopul's secret.

—You want to get me killed?

—He is eating that side, on the main street. He'll be gone for at least an hour. Come on, Farhad, you promised.

The Madina Orphanage sends some of the older, upper caste boys to work at the masjid. God is good and sows His gifts with a generous hand. While Farhad is slight, with un-warrior-like wide, hazel eyes, he is quick and intelligent. It is three years since the imam started his training in the copying of holy text. He can now copy text onto rolls of sheets brought by the man who drives a dirty jeep from across the border.

It is the first jeep Farhad has seen. It is the first jeep the imam has seen, too, but that is something they cannot discuss. The driver never speaks. There is no language for what he does, just as there is no language for what the artists do with those intricate gold and silver and blue letters like scattered treasure across the pages. Farhad longs to be the driver, or even his assistant, never speaking, eating three-day-old chapatis, delivering packages into the soft hands of the imams across the border.

In the waking world, Farhad is proud of having discovered

this hidden thing of Bhopul's. He wants to show his friends
that he, too, can be daring. He wishes to impress Hunri-Howri, who looks as though he could fight anyone, or drive a jeep,
even if he is only Shudra.

The three boys walk behind the hut, along another wet grass
path to a similar hut with a corrugated iron roof. Like all
doors in the village, Bhopul's is unlocked. Farhad kneels on
the floor by the cot and pulls out a grey and white goatskin
bag. He lifts it carefully onto the small writing desk. Inside
the bag, beneath a green cloth, is an old gun with a long, thin
barrel. Farhad stands back.

Sadiq, is thrilled and scared,

—What is he doing with a gun?

Hunri-Howri laughs,

—That's not a real gun. Real guns are short here.

He points at the barrel,

—And they are very shiny. I have seen it in a fillum. Look
at this thing—it's almost falling apart.

The door pushes open behind them and Bhopul stands
there, his chicken-grease moustache like a melting candle.
He would like to shout at them, but that would attract attention and, perhaps, even the imam might come. He regrets his
arrangement with the Dinkar, the chicken tikka seller—free
lunches in return for a matter of safe-keeping.

The grease drops on Bhopul's moustache quiver as he
tries to control his temper as he whispers,

—What are you doing? Hah? You will be put in jail one
time. Finish. I will teach you a lesson. So interested in the
gun, hah? *You* hold it.

He grabs it from its cloth nest and pushes it into Farhad's hand. Farhad jumps as though electrocuted and drops the gun. It hits the edge of the desk and there is an explosion. Sadiq jumps back, shoulders jarred against the wall. Dangling on a bent nail above the doorway, the jagged fragment of Bhopul's shaving mirror shivers, its sharp silver point trembling, falls like a star, a carelessly thrown dagger.

There is no sound, no movement, no light. Then Hunri-Howri hears coughing and sees Farhad on his knees, retching onto the brown blanket on Bhopul's cot. Sadiq is also on the floor, sitting in a strange, squashed up position against the wall. There is something that sparkles on his neck.

Hunri Howri kneels down,

—Sadiq?

Sadiq looks at Hunri-Howri, but does not speak.

The hut explodes with anxious voices, and arms pushing to get in. Someone stands on Farhad's left hand and he cries out. They see Sadiq, who opens his mouth. No sound. Someone says, *There now, Sadiqui.* There is a fractal movement of arms and backs as Sadiq is carried away, the mirror shard in his neck gummy with dark blood.

A few remain in the hut. Farhad sits with his arms tight around his knees. Hunri-Howri stares at Bhopul,

—Why do you keep this gun?

The gun lies on the floor pointing its dark eye at Hunri-Howri.

Bhopul says,

—Don't speak to me like that. It's your fault, good for nothing shanty boy.

Where the Birds Are

He turns to the others,

—He has come here for stealing and shooting guns.

Hunri-Howri feels them watching him. Someone will have to be blamed; such a thing can't just be an accident.

The *nazir* will say, *Tell me what happened.* Someone must suffer for this terrible injury to the son of one of the village councilmen. Hunri-Howri has no mother, a drunk father, and one stolen chapati. Perhaps the *nazir* will believe him and not Bhopul. It doesn't seem likely.

Outside, the mist is thickening. To the west there is a brighter part of the sky, as though the sun is trying to break through. He imagines what it is like behind the clouds, where the sun is bright, where the birds are, where you can see far across the world to the calm, green hills of Mumbai where he had an aunty. He saw a picture of her, once, in a red and silver sari. His mother once told him that the aunty loved him.

Kitchen Nerves

It is early evening, that time when I turn to my stove and wonder whether one more microwave meal will really kill us. And then decide maybe it will.

I am not a good cook; I have none of that fine, artistic manner I so admire in the TV chefs who sprinkle kosher salt and toss in shrimp and ginger without having to check the recipe. My recipes are in nice, plastic sheets so they sponge clean. I am a bit of a renegade in my own way: I always double the required garlic and add an extra sprig or two of basil, mint, lavender.

I am trying not to think of anything in particular when I open the oven door and think of you. You are far away and I don't suppose your immediate thoughts are about what you'll be cooking for dinner. I suppose there must be someone else responsible for food. Will you have any variation in diet or will it be the equivalent of a hunk of bread and a bowl of water? Will they let you drink from a bowl? I can't imagine you drinking from a bowl. You never even drank your cereal milk from the bowl, even though I showed you how. Of course, that was a long time ago, at least fourteen years.

Now you're nineteen; that's a two-syllable word I'm not afraid of. I always thought it would be a single syllable that would crush me, like someone dropping a brick on my head. Shot. Bombed. Dead. But now the terror has exploded my nightmares with two syllables: captured.

And that means they wanted you alive. Your dad said I was talking crazy about why couldn't they have just shot you.

I set the oven to broil. Now, where did I put the bell peppers? Here they are in the lower drawer of the fridge. One red, one yellow. Festive colors; the kind you see in photographs of Indian women in saris, or Mexican women hanging rugs, or African women in arid villages where red and yellow jeeps drive past on their way to the tourist resorts.

You're in Africa; North Africa, you might say, although they don't call it that. You were always so quick with languages: German, Russian, French. None of those will help you there. I wonder if you can speak any of the language. I wonder if you are permitted to speak at all.

Tonight, we're having Chicken Provençale. It's an old recipe and I haven't sponged the plastic sheet clean because the stains are from the last time I cooked it. That's when you helped me cut up the tomatoes. It was in the summer and we had far too many for the recipe, so we started by eating a couple and then we had a tomato fight. You lobbed one at my head and said it was great hair conditioner. I got you on the back of your neck and it slid right down inside your shirt. We were still cleaning up when your Dad came home. He just shook his head. *I hope you haven't spoiled the dinner.*

I'll cut the chicken up first. It's what they call chicken

breast fillets. This means the original chicken parts have been shaved into half-inch slabs. I carve them into what I think the recipe means by 'morsels.' Small, pink, skinned fingers of flesh. They look so bare. I push them into a heap on one side of the chopping board.

I open the oven and place the peppers on the rack. After they've roasted, I'll put them in a paper bag until I can shuck their skins.

Now for the tomatoes; they are also to lose their skins. I put a pan of water on to boil.

There isn't anything left to do but I need something to keep me occupied while I wait. I'll make a salad; a bag of chopped romaine, sliced green apple, some broken pecans, lime and honey dressing. It sounds green and exotic.

I wonder if they pick limes or pecans from the trees, wherever you are. Even if you don't get any, I'm sure you can probably see them. From wherever you are. I like to imagine you're in some place with palm trees above to remind you of home. That's about all that will remind you of home.

Perhaps you can look up and see the stars between the palm fronds. Perhaps you can roast fresh cashew nuts over the fire, and think of us. You have to allow me some creative thinking here, since I don't know what's actually going on over there. But I do know the stars are white and milky and too many to count.

Like when we used to go to Owens River Gorge. You and your climbing, Dad and his fishing, me trailing behind one or the other of you with caution trapped behind my teeth. Not too far, not too deep, not too high. Don't trust the rope, the reel, the belayer, the net.

But at night—remember? Oh at night, it didn't matter, all of the worrying, the anticipation of something going wrong—all that was gone as we three sat back in our chairs and just looked up. I had no idea what the constellations were. There I was enthusiastically pointing out the Big Bear and Orion, and you and Dad laughing hysterically because I was pointing in the wrong direction.

I didn't care, though. I dragged out that enormous box of Maltesers I got from the duty-free store on our way back through Heathrow over Christmas.

And you said,

—You're the best, mom.

Dad said,

—Can't tell a star from a stop sign, but she's all right.

And you hugged me and said,

—Don't pay attention to *him*. You're more than all right.

I made sure you weren't too close to the fire, and I hugged you back. You were so tall, even then. Well, I don't suppose I'm much of a judge, being five foot one. But I had to reach up to hug you properly. You were sixteen.

I can smell the peppers burning. Cooking. I take a look inside the oven. The skin is blistering and popping. It's going black. They're only peppers. You're supposed to cook them like this. They taste great cooked like this. I try to shut out the thought that it must take a long time to broil a human, and shut the oven door.

The water for the tomatoes is boiling and I turn off the heat and ease the tomatoes in. The skin separates. I can't look at them. I put the lid on the pan.

I sprinkle salt and pepper over the chicken. I can't bring

myself to rub it all in. It's not the slimy feel of the raw chicken, it's the rubbing the salt and pepper into the flesh. I put a towel over the chicken.

I turn the peppers, using the tongs. I should have used a tray. The juice is dripping onto the floor of the oven. It'll burn into a charred scar and I'll never be able to scrub it out.

Those oven cleaners are meant to be very efficient, but they just burn everything away. Burning out the burns.

I try reading the paper while the peppers finish cooking. I keep reading the same paragraph over and over. I'm too nervous to let the peppers be, so I check them before they're ready to be turned. I see their skins pop and bubble. I watch the stalks blacken. How long they take to broil, and they're so small.

I read about the weather on the back of the paper. I look at the yellow dots that mean the air is unhealthy for sensitive people. There's one orange dot on Riverside and that means the air is unhealthy for everyone.

What's the air like where you are? I hope you're breathing okay. I hope you have fresh air. It's meant to be very healthy around plants and I know you've got some of those. I've seen them on TV.

The peppers are done and I drop their poor, depleted shapes into the paper bag. They're not bright and firm anymore. It seems half of their insides are sizzling at the bottom of the oven.

I take the tomatoes out and put them on the chopping board. The skins peel off easily and the flesh underneath is soft and spongy. I cut the tomatoes up and remove the seeds. There's hardly anything left.

Now to cook the chicken. They call it sautéing, but it just means frying. I heat the skillet and pour in a little oil. It skids about on the bottom of the pan. What would it be like to place my hand there? How long could I hold it?

I tip the chopping board and the chicken hisses and spits as it hits the oil. I stir it quickly and add two pinches of saffron. The chicken turns white then yellow as the saffron threads melt.

I open the paper bag and pull out the charred peppers. I run them under the cold water and peel off the blackened skins. The stalks, seeds and membranes come away easily. They look nothing like peppers anymore. I add them and the tomatoes to the chicken. Now it looks like food. I can feel myself unclenching.

I can imagine you coming through the front door,

—What's cooking, mom? Smells good.

And I'd tell you to get a bowl and I'd heap it high and cut you two slabs of bread so you could soak up the sauce. And we'd sit opposite each other, eating like crazy until it was all gone. And I'd say,

—What am I going to feed your father?

And you'd say,

—We'll just get pizza.

And we're laughing and going back into the kitchen, and tearing off bits of bread to scoop up the last bit of sauce from the pan. And we don't burn our fingers.

And you're so real, and firm and bright, it just isn't possible that you've melted away into something I might not recognize.

Author

Sandra Hunter's fiction won the 2016 Gold Line Press Chapbook Prize, October 2014 Africa Book Club Award, and three Pushcart Prize nominations. Her story "Finger Popping" won second place in the 2017 Katherine Anne Porter Prize in Short Fiction. She is a 2018 Hawthornden Fellow and the 2017 Charlotte Sheedy Fellow at the MacDowell Colony. The short fiction chapbook, *Small Change*, was published in August 2016 and her debut novel, *Losing Touch,* was published in 2014. She's just finished her second novel, *The Geography of Kitchen Tables*, set in post-apartheid South Africa, and is working on the sequel, *Fissures of Men*. Sandra Hunter lives in Ventura, California where she teaches English and Creative Writing and runs writing workshops. She is represented by Writers House.

Interview

Andrew Fairweather is a librarian with the New York Public Library, Seward Park Branch (www.npyl.org/about/locations/seward-park). He interviewed Sandra Hunter about *Trip Wires*, raising questions about identity and immigration.

Andrew Fairweather: I feel that 'Against the Stranger' was an excellent way to introduce *Trip Wires*, with the awkward yet charming relationship between the American soldier, Tak, and the boy, Hamasa, served to illustrated Tak's own tension in regards to his own heritage not far from the Afghanistan border where the story takes place. Throughout the story, Tak's feelings toward his troop, his father, and Hamasa seem unsettled. In the end, the soldier and the boy are literally brought closer by the blood they spill through experiencing a shared, violent trauma. How significant is it that this story served to introduce the collection?

Sandra Hunter: Thank you. It was important that this piece start the collection because identity is set against violence that can arise out of nowhere. Who are we now? Who are we in five minutes? Who are we before and after a violent event that happens to us, to someone we know, to a stranger? I'm interested in that moment of change, and often a personal connection in that moment of change. This story has an engaging and difficult moment of change. I felt this story set up the rest of the collection in its extremes: the location, the situation, the threat and occurrence of violence, and the aftermath.

"Against the Stranger" works, I hope, on several levels of the sense of self. Tak is both American and Pakistani. When we meet him he's in uniform, clearly a US soldier but his Pakistani heritage is immediately identified by Hamasa, the young Afghani boy who becomes his friend. There's also the level of how Tak is seen by his army buddies, some of whom casually call him "dune coon." Then there is Tak's complex relationship with his father who completely identifies with his Pakistani roots but also insists that Tak join the US Army so that he can go to college "like all the men in our family." Until this peace-keeping mission, Tak has thought of himself as American, but in the face of these conflicting identities he is no longer sure.

AF: From what I've read in *Trip Wires*, and from what you've just told me, "culture" and "belonging" seem to be at the forefront of what is being reflected upon in this collection. Is this fair?

SH: Absolutely. Culture and belonging are rooted in my personal experience, so here goes! I was born in England

and shared my Indian parents' fear of being singled out for looking different. My parents tried to look as British as possible. I went further and tried to be invisible. I would walk on the extreme inside or outside of the pavement so people coming towards me wouldn't have to see me and launch the usual "nigger" or "paki" insult.

I grew up and went to college, shared a love of books and music with friends, and accreted British culture: mistrust of anyone who appeared confident, a love of complaining about the weather, a muscular endurance for standing in queues, and also, a tendency to be wary of Indians. So, I was British.

But in the 1980s when I worked in Kenya for two years I had time to think about myself as I settled into a new culture in Kisii, a region southwest of Nairobi. I thought about what I still considered "home." There was little electricity in rural Kenya, so this meant no TV or radio in the evenings. I talked to people and read (a lot) by the light of hurricane lanterns.

When I came back to England, reverse culture shock had the effect of clarifying that I didn't belong. I was Sri Lankan with Dutch and Portuguese ancestors. I was Anglo-Indian with a great grandfather from Scotland. I had worked in Switzerland and spoke French. I had lived in Kenya and spoke Swahili and Kisii. This is not unique. Many people belong to a range of cultures, and are perfectly comfortable. Somehow, I wasn't.

AF: Ah, your experience sounds like a parallel to Tak's insofar as his being removed from his native culture, "American," helped strengthen his relationship to his ethnic, or paternal culture . . . or is this too simple?

SH: You're right—there's a definite parallel. But I think Tak's sense of his American self highlights his separation from his father, despite their closeness and his longing for a sense of family. The sense of rootlessness is far more central to the story. The liminal has informed much of my fiction. In "A Nigerian in Paris," "15 Minutes," or "Angel in Glasgow," a character is introduced into a western culture where all the life rhythms are different: social languages, humor, even walking. In "Radio Radio," "Borderland," and "Where the Birds Are," the setting itself can function as the antagonist. This has the effect of disorienting the characters and may even place them in danger. Tak feels he's armed and defended but he's actually much more vulnerable than the people still living in the bombed-out village and, as the story progresses, this begins to uproot his sense of ethnic identity.

Moments of belonging are infrequent and often ephemeral. But when they occur, they are vivid and dimensional and inclusive. Those instances of deep connection—or at least deeper than the social road-drill exchanges that pass for conversation—are like phosphorescence, where you see the world, even briefly, in a uniquely illuminated way.

AF: Why did this need to be a work of fiction? Do you feel that fiction was better suited to deliver a more complex cross-cultural portrait than, say, a simple interview with subjects displaced by violence?

Interview

SH: Well, it's the story that interests me! I'm fascinated by dialogue: what people reveal intentionally and, more interestingly, what they conceal. In nonfiction the limitations are obvious. The events and interactions are observed or they're not. With fiction any moment—historically significant or not—can be expanded and inhabited by real or imaginary characters. For example, Robert Graves' *I, Claudius*. Here we meet Tiberius and Julius Caesar and the manipulative Livia and the completely insane Caligula—and they're dimensional: narcissistic, absolutely bananas about power, and utterly compelling. They leap off the page and force you to pay attention. The Kardashians are pale, limp wannabes by comparison. The book was immensely popular long before the TV series.

Graves also translated Suetonius' *The Twelve Caesars*. The period and people are well-portrayed and the book has his compelling world-evoking style, but it doesn't have the dramatic scope of *I, Claudius*. Dickens did great things for Victorian history, the novels ricocheting and shuddering with his characters' voices, and in the background he lobs insights into child labor and exploitation, or the Marshalsea, reflecting his interest in social reform. So the fiction writer can ask questions and draw conclusions within an historical period without being relentlessly stapled to a specific chronology of historical facts.

AF: Yes, and in a similar way, the issue of diversity seems to be at the front lines of our own historical moment, and *Trip Wires* strikes me as a collection not afraid to go amongst the weeds. I feel that the collection contains many examples of characters who are limited in their capacity to function as effective interlocutors with "the stranger." I'm not sure whether this was something you were thinking about when writing this collection—but the stories do seem to disclose something richer than a voyeuristic, non-fiction approach with pretensions to having access to a sort of raw truth.

SH: In these stories, the "raw truth" is brought by the reader. For example, the characters may not be aware of the beginning of the anti-government protests in Syria in 2011, or the suicide protests in Abu Ghraib, or the civil war in the Sudan—but the reader may be. And if they aren't, perhaps they may Google that information. Our presence in dialogue is determined partly by a lack of knowledge or perspective that may be provided by the other party, or may be undisclosed and discovered at a later time. It continues whether or not the two parties are literally engaged. Dialogue can be between the interlocutor and geographical or time-related setting or with political unrest, or the aftermath of disaster, or silence. The reader's engagement is what makes the stories have impact. Ondaatje once said that the writer provides 80% and the reader supplies 20%. I'm hoping that the 20% includes a world awareness. I'm also interested in the interrogation of the self. What is the perception of reality of identity? In "Fifteen Minutes," who is Asal in that moment when her apparently-dead phone rings? She says, "There was a time when I was a modern girl": how does she see herself at that point in her memory compared to where she is now, "a married woman with a child"? Farid draws on memory to prepare himself for death: how does memory alter the sense of what is true and how much reality is present in memory? How is memory altered or constructed? What we remember is overlaid with emotion. How essential is it to have historically accurate memories?

AF: These events like the protests in 2011 and so on that the reader may or may not be aware of . . . was *Trip Wires* written in response to any particular event or series of events?

SH: The stories were written and published in various magazines over the years. In fact, I didn't realize that there was this common thread of threatened identity for some time. I'd respond to a news report about some atrocity or disaster and I'd usually get incredibly angry, which would spark some character or moment in the story that would begin to develop. As an entity, the collection is more of an ongoing investigation of the persistence of human cruelty or neglect juxtaposed against human resilience, generosity, and compassion.

However, recently it does seem that there has been an intensifying of focus on singular interests: the pipeline, the wall, the relentless investment in the search for oil resources, tax breaks for corporations. Perhaps the focus hasn't been intensifying: it's just that this kind of focus is now an accepted part of contemporary conversation, coupled with the fact that the internet and social media make such focus more accessible.

AF: I felt that the children in the story often served as a promise of regeneration towards a better world. What is your understanding of childhood, and to what extent did it inform your process in writing these stories?

SH: This isn't necessarily about children being the future, but it does demonstrate that children represent the best of us. Their response to hardship is to survive and protect those they love, often at a high cost to themselves. My understanding of childhood has certain points of interest to me: vulnerability, cunning, endless imagination, for example. But childhood situated in difficult circumstances is varied in how survival occurs.

AF: I see. Let me try to think of an example of what I was getting at. As I read it, unlike the children, many of the adult characters are trying to outpace past violence—a vivid example is 'Borderland' which features a family on the run from some murky violence which catches up with them on the border. Yet, the of cycle violence is stanched by the refugee's child who serves as a point of contact between Marta, the runaway, and Telik, the soldier, two women who are strangers to one another. How did you understand this reprieve of violence in this story as it related to the child?

SH: For much of the story we see Marta and Ticho and, to some extent, Israel, as the victims of a pitiless administration. The patrol makes its first appearance when the train, on which Marta and Ticho are traveling, is blown up. The patrol attempts to kill everyone on board. Later on, another

patrol soldier, Telik, is revealed first as a woman and sec-
ondly as a wife who has lost her husband in the exchange
of gunfire. We also learn that Telik once had a child. We
don't know what happened to it, whether it died or was tak-
en from Telik once she was recruited to the patrol. We find
out that the third soldier is also a woman who was going to
kill Ticho before Telik shot her. The shared maternal experience is what makes Telik shoot the third soldier. Despite
her role as a border protector, she cannot allow Ticho to be
killed. This decision forces her to cross a line—a border
of sorts—which then becomes literal as she (also literally) lays down her life so Marta can escape. Ticho, then, is
the catalyst for Telik's decision. She also knows that more
patrol soldiers are coming and she will be shot for failing
to stop Marta and Ticho from crossing.

AF: Much of the substance of the characters in *Trip Wires*
strikes me as defined by the breadth of choices they have
or have not been able to make thus far; that is, whether
they've been thus far trapped in a world not of their own
making, or regarded the world as a series of choices. Did
you think about "choices" when you wrote these stories?

SH: Most of the choices the characters make are forced
on them by circumstances, such as war or predators. There
has to be change and, I hope, regeneration. When there is
a violent upheaval such as an earthquake, the topography
is changed. It's possible to argue that the topology changes
since the spaces in and between things have also changed.
Therefore what is known is also changed. This street no

longer connects to that avenue and so on. But the deeper changes are also connected to memory: the definition of place as envisioned by the individual. It falls to the individual to adapt. Children are excellent adapters and so they do represent hope.

AF: I like the analogy you made between earthquakes and topology, and trauma. What takes place is an entire re-orientation of the mind. So yes, I can understand this sense of children representing hope. The adults, on the other hand, suffer from an overwhelming estrangement, a condition exhibited by many of the characters in *Trip Wires* . . . even the so-called natives, like Indira in "My Brother's Keeper," seem estranged, perhaps from herself? After all, Elijah, the refugee, is very aware that he is assisting Indira in her own perception of herself as his savior. Kenzie and Sheila, the native Glaswegians in "Angel in Glasgow" are spontaneous and bold in their actions, yet hopelessly lost from one moment to the next. Do you feel that this is an accurate assessment?

SH: There's a discomfort with the self that is reflected in these conflicted situations. This may be a result of the barrage of media and internet, the shift towards a singular projection of "success," the helpless knowledge that, according to social standards, 99.9% of us will never be "enough." The dire circumstances of the characters reflect radically imbalanced socio-political situations, but there is also a reference to the more privileged citizens. In "My Brother's Keeper." Indira has the appearance of balance. She is affluent and poised but has a flimsy grasp of self-knowledge. She isn't comfortable with herself, her children, and definitely not with Elijah. The characters who are most deeply threatened appear to have an awareness of themselves and their experiences. Hunri Howri ("Where The Birds Are") is resigned to the fact that there must be a scapegoat and it will be him. By contrast, Indira and even Asal ("Fifteen Minutes") do not have this kind of self-awareness.

AF: Interesting. What do you think accounts for the poise of the characters who are most under threat in these stories? Is it a matter of their having to be more flexible with their idea of themselves, or something like that?

SH: They react to situations with the practical need for survival. When the soldiers come, Elijah pushes his small brother out of the back window and tells him to run to his uncle's house. If Elijah hadn't been quick-witted, his brother may have died. That's the difference: the ones who react quickly become narrators. Conversely, the woman narrator in "Kitchen Nerves" reacts less in the delicate moment before the panic actually strikes, probably because there's nothing she can actually do.

Perhaps that's what you mean—these quiet moments when the characters contemplate themselves and what will happen next. There's an interiority that requires them to achieve more than they have previously, whether it's to go through with a suicide or the decision to go back to a war-torn country in search of a brother.

AF: In this collection there's often a dichotomy between the gritty, oppressive actual and the joyful promise the future might hold. Do you feel that childhood, motherhood, and the suppression of women in traditionalist cultures is, in a way, a suppression of a future which might challenge the dominant power structure?

SH: Well, yes, but that isn't the central intention in the collection. The "joyful promise" is more in the moment rather than some nebulous "future." Circumstances for these characters are precarious. They can only move from this moment to this moment. Even Dilan, in "Radio Radio," who is no longer a captive, has not moved past the moment-by-moment life. He can only wake up and clean the cobwebs from the sink. He can walk down a street with a bag. He cannot look far enough into the future to imagine seeing his mother face to face.

For these characters, the concept of "future" has been almost irrevocably telescoped. For Marta and Ticho, for Minoo ("Angel in Glasgow"), and the unnamed mother in "Kitchen Nerves," there is only learning how to breathe through the now. In graphic novels, it's called time decompression, a deceleration so that the reader might be aware of how the characters move through these incremental moments of change.

AF: Do you imagine that you'll continue to write stories along similar themes found in *Trip Wires* or do you feel that this collection is a capstone on a certain trajectory of your writing so far?

Interview

SH: Oh dear. I have no clue! I think this collection has done what it needs to do. Future writings may include more stories in a child's voice in a turbulent setting—and god knows there are plenty of those stories out there in the world—but I don't think it will be a deliberate focus.

AF: What sort of work, fiction or non-fiction, do you tend to gravitate toward as a reader, and does it bear any relation to what you like to write?

SH: Chris Abani. Percival Everett. Mary Rakow. I also love writing by women travelers like Mary Kingsley and Freya Stark. Then there's Tomas Transtromer, Lesego Rampolokeng, Safiya Sinclair and Ilya Kaminsky. How much time do you have?

All the books I read have some bearing on what I write, directly or not. The poets are especially inspiring if I'm stuck somewhere. Even if it seems the book has no relevance to a current project, something will wriggle its way into my brain and pop out when I'm least expecting it.

Questions for Reading Groups

We hope the following questions will enhance your group's discussion on youth around the world who confront impossible odds. These stories will take you to Afghanistan, Los Angeles, Syria, Abu Ghraib, Glasgow, Colombia, Paris, India, the US, and an unknown dystopian future, where young people, with virtually no resources struggle to find creative ways out of their dilemmas with compassion and genuine love for one another.

General

1. Discuss the title and its possible meanings.
2. Do you think the cover predicts what the book is about?
3. What did you like best/least about the stories?
4. A number of the stories are written from a child's viewpoint. Do you think these voices are believable?
5. Discuss the realism of the story world, characters, relationships, and dilemmas.
6. What's a favorite quote from any of the stories?

7. What do you think fiction reveals about culture and history that memoir or history books cannot?
8. How are cultural identities shaped during political, military, economic and religious power struggles?
9. How is the concept of family transformed for the immigrant or the war survivor?
10. Despite the difficult, often brutal, circumstances for the characters, do you think the author includes hope?

Against the Stranger

11. What did you know about the 2017 military exchange between Pakistani and Afghani security forces before you read this story?
12. Discuss the title and the epigraph.
13. Do you think the relationship of Tak and his father has any effect on Tak's friendship with Hamasa?
14. Tak thinks Hamasa's a typical kid wanting American candy. What insight does the real reason—selling the candy—give you about these kids?
15. Do you think anyone dies at the end of the story?

Brother's Keeper

16. Which of the two narrators, Indira and Elijah, do you find more believable?
17. Which character do you like best/least?
18. If Elijah had decided to stay, what do you think the ending might have been?
19. Can you imagine what it will be like for Elijah going

back to Southern Sudan? Will it be dangerous or just difficult?

20. Do you think Elijah will find his brother?

Modern Jazz Parade

21. Did you guess from the story that it's set around the beginning of the anti-government protests in Syria in 2011?
22. Discuss the title and the use of music in the story.
23. Do Basem and his best friend Ziad remind you of anyone you know?
24. Who's your favorite character?
25. Traditionally, it's the big brother's job to protect the little sister. In this story, the roles are reversed. Discuss how this happens and why.

Fifteen Minutes

26. What did you know about Abu Ghraib and the protest suicides before you read this story?
27. Discuss how time moves differently for Asal and Farid.
28. If someone had spoken when Asal answered her phone, what do you think might have happened?
29. Do you think Asal will stay in America?
30. Why does Farid say "Goodbye. Forgive me"?

Angel in Glasgow

31. What did you know about the civil war in Sudan be-

fore you read this story?

32. What do Minoo's memories say about her hopes and fears?
33. If Minoo hadn't left the family she's been living with what might have happened?
34. Kenzie, a native Glaswegian, and Sheila, from Liverpool, speak with strong accents. Minoo's accent appears to change at the end of the story. Discuss the use of accents.
35. Who's your favorite/least favorite character?

Radio Radio

36. What do you imagine it is like at Voces del Secuestro while the families are waiting their turn to speak to their kidnapped loved ones?
37. Discuss Dilan's relationship with his mother.
38. The story examines forgiveness. Is there something/someone you can't forgive?
39. What is Dilan's key to survival?
40. Do you think Dilan will adjust to his new-found freedom in Caracas?

Borderland

41. What physical sense of the country do you get? Does it remind you of anywhere you've been?
42. What is revealed about women? Do you think Marta realizes anything about herself?
43. Do you think you could do what Marta did if your life depended on it?

Questions for Reading Groups

44. Do you think the family is safe across the border?
45. Which of the characters do you like/dislike?

A Nigerian in Paris

46. Bem's family was killed and he was drafted as a child soldier. How do you think he copes now that he's in Paris? Do you think he can adjust to society?
47. What character appeals to you most?
48. One of Bem's most revealing moments is when he takes a shower. Have you ever had to go without showering for a few days?
49. The story discusses the issue of a racial pecking order: Miriam and Patrice are brown, so they consider they are superior to Bem. Why?
50. At the end of the story, Bem recognizes the importance of his name. What is the importance of your name?

Where the Birds Are

51. In this remote Punjabi village (North West India) they are feeling the effects of a recent bombing. Discuss the impact of war on innocents.
52. What character do you like/dislike?
53. Are the voices of the children believable?
54. What did you know about the Indian caste system before you read this story?
55. What might have happened if the mirror shard had fallen on Hunri-Howri instead of Sadiq?

Sandra Hunter

Kitchen Nerves

56. Is the voice of this character believable?
57. What the narrator doesn't know is as disturbing as what she does know. Discuss this idea of knowing and not knowing.
58. How does the narrator's preparation of dinner expose her anguish?
59. Discuss the use of memory to block tragedy.